Montana Cowboy Bride

Montana Cowboy Bride

A Wyatt Brothers Romance

Jane Porter

Montana Cowboy Bride
Copyright© 2023 Jane Porter
Tule Publishing First Printing, April 2023

The Tule Publishing, Inc.

ALL RIGHTS RESERVED

First Publication by Tule Publishing 2023

Cover design by Lee Hyat at www.LeeHyat.com

No part of this book may be used or reproduced in any manner whatsoever without written permission except in the case of brief quotations embodied in critical articles and reviews.

This is a work of fiction. Names, characters, places, and incidents are products of the author's imagination or are used fictitiously. Any resemblance to actual events, locales, organizations, or persons, living or dead, is entirely coincidental.

ISBN: 978-1-959988-60-1

Dedication

Monti Shalosky
This one is for you!

Prologue

New Year's Day, Wyoming

BRIAR PHILLIPS HAD driven all night to reach the Sundowner Ranch from her home in Paradise Valley, Montana. Her dad thought she was at a New Year's Eve party. Instead, she was on the highway with a full tank of gas and a turkey and cheese sandwich she'd picked up inside the gas station's mini market. She'd only discovered where her half brother was a day ago. Now that she knew Cade Hunt managed the Sundowner, she tossed an overnight bag into the car and went.

It didn't matter that the weather wasn't the best. It didn't matter that it was the holidays. It didn't matter that he was in Wyoming and not Montana. She just had to find him. She'd been looking for him forever.

But now that she was at the Sundowner and one of the bleary-eyed cowboys outside pointed her to an old log cabin, she was finally meeting him, finally face-to-face.

She'd surprised him at the door, and he invited her in, saying it had been a big night. They'd recently welcomed a baby.

Clearly, she'd come at the wrong time, but she'd been waiting years to meet him. Years to find family that was hers, that she belonged to ... genetics, DNA, home.

But now that she was face-to-face with him, Briar wasn't sure what to feel. Cade didn't look anything like her. He was very tall and broad through the shoulders. He had a big frame, strong face with a square jaw. She was a brunette, but he was fair, with thick sandy-blond hair, light eyes, and a firm mouth that didn't seem as if it knew how to smile.

Cade introduced her to his wife, MerriBee, and their new baby, and then MerriBee and the baby disappeared into the bedroom, and Cade had Briar join him in the kitchen as he made a fresh pot of coffee. "This is a shock," he said.

"I probably should have warned you," she said, "but once I knew where you were, I couldn't stay away."

"I'm glad you're here," he said, facing her.

She searched his expression wondering if that was how he truly felt. "It's taken me a long time to find you." She tried to make it a joke. "Were you hiding?"

"No."

He didn't get the joke and her desire to smile faded. "Why did you change your name? I'd spent two years looking for a Cade O'Connell—"

"I changed it after Mom died and I found out that my stepfather was just my stepfather and not my dad." He gestured to the coffeepot now brewing. "I didn't even ask if you wanted coffee. Would you prefer something else? Tea, a soda, water?"

"Coffee's great. My favorite drink."

"Mom used to drink a lot of it, too," Cade said.

"Really?" Briar glanced around the log cabin, wondering if there were any pictures of their mom. "I know nothing about her. She left me a letter. I got to read it when I was eighteen. She told me in the letter about you. She said her husband Jimmy wasn't my dad so I couldn't live with them."

"Jimmy wasn't my dad either and was a horrible human being. You're lucky to have been raised somewhere else."

"It was that bad?"

Cade nodded.

She swallowed, uncertain why a lump filled her throat. "Do you have any photos of Suzy? Our mom?"

"I have a couple but they're all in storage. We recently converted the spare room into the baby's room and so a lot of things ended up in boxes in the attic."

"You must miss her," Briar said.

He shrugged. "She wasn't happy, and then she wasn't well. She's probably better where she is—"

"Dead?" Briar interrupted, shocked.

"Out of pain," he said. "No longer suffering."

The heaviness returned to Briar, sinking in her, from her shoulders to her chest and down into her belly. "Did I do that to her?"

Cade grabbed two mugs from an open shelf and filled them with coffee. "Why would you think that?"

"You said she wasn't happy. That she was suffering."

"Did she regret giving you up? Probably. But I don't think she had any other choice. She did what she did to give you a better life." He handed her the coffee and then gestured to the bruise on her cheek.

It took Briar a moment to understand, and she lifted her hand, lightly touching her cheek. She'd forgotten all about the mark. "Oh, no. That's nothing. You should have seen it two weeks ago."

"It's a pretty ugly bruise. Takes up half your face."

"Hardly. I should have known better. I was being impatient."

"Impatient doing what?"

"Training. I work with horses. I like horses. Probably the only thing I like."

He lifted an eyebrow. "Bad home life?"

"*No*. My parents are great. I shouldn't complain about them. I shouldn't have anything to complain about."

"But you do."

Suddenly her chest tightened, and she couldn't breathe. "Are there some things I'd change? Yes. My mom passed away when I was in high school, and I wish she was still with us today. My dad's a really good man, and he tries hard, but he misses her terribly and I haven't been easy on him."

"That's part of being a teenager. But you're growing up, growing out of it now."

She nodded but the emotion was hitting hard, so much

emotion. She'd been looking for her brother for so many years and he didn't seem all that excited to see her. Perhaps she'd expected too much, wanting so badly to have family that was connected by blood. She didn't know why it mattered but for most of her life Briar had just felt out of step ... different. Problematic. She'd hoped finding Cade would help ease some of that emptiness. Instead, she felt even more alone.

"What's wrong?" Cade asked, his blue gaze narrowing.

She shook her head, forced a smile, not wanting to be an emotional wreck already. Her brother was thirteen years older and had grown up in a tough family and he didn't need a half sister to show up bawling on his doorstep. "Just glad to finally find you," she said huskily, smiling bigger, hoping the smile would hold back tears.

"Not that it's a competition," he said, jaw easing, his expression warmer. "I've been looking for you a long time, too. I've been looking for you even longer than you've been looking for me. I've been worried about you, worried you weren't in a good situation, worried you needed me and I was nowhere to be found."

"My family couldn't have been nicer. My dad, Patrick, is a pastor. My mom, Joany, was one of the best human beings on this planet. I guess that's why God needed her back." Briar swallowed hard, a lump filling her throat. She studied Cade carefully, trying to see a family resemblance. She wasn't finding what she'd hoped to find in his face. "Do you look like Mom … our mom?"

"No," he said. "But she was beautiful."

"She was?"

He nodded, expression somber.

His expression made her chest tighten and ache and her eyes sting, hot and gritty. "What did she look like?"

"You," Cade said almost grimly. "Just like you."

Chapter One

THE FIRST TIME Briar Phillips showed up at the Sundowner Ranch, was also the last time.

It had been a little over a year ago and she'd been desperate and emotional, angry and broken. She didn't know what she wanted from her older brother Cade, except he hadn't given it to her, and by the time she left three days later, she wished she'd never found him. She'd dreamed about meeting him for so many years that when she came face-to-face with him, and discovered he was a cool, cryptic cowboy she snapped. She'd needed unconditional love and acceptance, but instead, Cade played the heavy, giving her advice she didn't want or need brother.

No, that first meeting over New Year's hadn't been encouraging, and when she'd left, she'd stormed off after telling him in no uncertain terms what she thought of him, and it wasn't flattering. She was certain she'd burned those bridges but when she'd gotten a birthday present six weeks later from Cade and MerriBee, the card glossed over the fallout, and wished her the happiest twenty-first birthday and sent lots of love.

Briar had been sure the gift was from MerriBee not Cade, but Cade's signature had been there at the bottom of the card, along with the scrawled message, *You're always welcome here, sis.*

Briar hadn't thought she'd return to the Sundowner anytime soon, but here she was, in her truck, with a suitcase and duffel bag, hauling her horse trailer—with horse.

She'd pretty much arrived at the ranch with everything she owned, and she wasn't angry and broken this time, but she wasn't happy, either. The truth was, she wasn't in a good place, and she didn't want or need help from anyone, she just needed some time to figure out her next move, a place that could have her and her horse. Briar had put herself in this situation and she'd figure out the next steps and with Dad in Australia as part of a cowboy church outreach, it seemed like a good time to head to Wyoming and come up with a plan without speculation from her dad's congregation, or Marietta busybodies.

Having been raised by good, kind, generous, God-loving parents, Briar knew right from wrong. She couldn't have asked for a better family, or a more caring family and knew what responsibility looked like and knew that as an adult what was expected of her. But she'd chosen a different path than the one her family would want for her. To be fair, it wasn't the path she'd wanted for herself, but she was on it now thanks to her own recklessness, and she'd had to live with the consequences as well.

Those consequences chiefly being a baby and her being single.

It wasn't the end of the world to be a single mother, but at the same time it added complications as generous measures of pain and regret.

Briar regretted creating pain for her father. She regretted making stupid choices. She regretted her immaturity and hotheadedness, and she *was* a hothead. She'd been a hothead her entire life. Her late mom used to joke that Briar had to be a redhead; that somewhere beneath all that dark brown hair, there was a little shock of red. But no, it was just Briar ... fierce, feisty, and foolishly independent.

From a very young age she'd wanted to do it *on my own*, and *by myself*. She could remember roaring at her parents to let her stir something by herself, without their help. She didn't remember if it was a brownie mix or pancakes, but she'd been stirring something with a wood spoon and making a huge mess and she hadn't wanted her mother to take the spoon back or try to slow her down. Her mother had been a saint, and she didn't get angry. Instead, she laughed and kissed the top of Briar's head, but the laughter didn't last as Briar grew older and continued to roar at them, demanding freedom and independence, insisting they let her be herself and refusing to be corralled or redirected. She was who she was and not their puppet or doll, and they'd have to accept it whether they liked it or not.

Parking the truck in an empty spot between Cade's cabin

and the ranch's big barn, she turned the engine off, feeling a sharp pinch of regret.

She hadn't been an easy daughter, and she'd tried their patience, and their faith, and that was something considering her father was a pastor, and a visible respected man of faith in the professional rodeo cowboy circuit. It couldn't have been easy for either her mom or dad being challenged right and left. Now with her mom gone, and just Dad remaining, Briar couldn't stay with him at her childhood home, getting bigger and bigger while her dad struggled to come to terms with her unplanned pregnancy, biting his tongue to hold back his fears, while nightly praying over her, wanting her to get right with the Lord.

No, remaining at home wasn't the answer, and while she tried to figure out the answer, she needed someplace to live, someplace her horse could live, someplace they could be together.

Briar drew the key from the ignition, took a deep breath, and stepped out of the truck, her boots crunching the combination of gravel, ice, and mud that covered the drive. The last snow had been weeks ago but the cold temperatures at night refroze whatever melted during the day, and while fresh snow was pretty, the dirty patches that remained weren't.

Briar peeked into her trailer, checked on Judas, and he nickered at her, his impatient let-me-out nicker, and she smiled grimly, feeling his pain.

Turning away, she walked quickly toward Cade and MerriBee's old log cabin, which had been one of the first buildings on the Wyoming property, constructed of old timber over one hundred and fifty years ago, one of the many facts Cade had told her as he took her on a tour of the Sundowner her first and only other time here. He'd been as proud of the place as if he owned it instead of managing it for a rich old lady who had never married or had kids. It was one of the things that had gotten Briar's back up—his devotion to this woman who wasn't family—and his brusqueness with her, Briar, who was family. She'd never had any biological family, no one who'd been hers, until him, and then he hadn't seemed to care one way or another.

And maybe that wasn't totally fair, because he'd been so happy to meet her, initially. But as the days passed, he didn't seem to like who she was. Maybe because she didn't like who she was, but that was in the past, and she was moving forward. Hopefully, Cade could move forward, too, because she needed a job.

Job hunting was problematic for her seeing as she had a high school diploma but not a lot of business skills. She was skilled with horses, though. She could ride, rope, and train horses, young, old, and everything in between. At home, she spent most of her time in the barn, or over at her neighbor's horse farm where she exercised the horses, cleaned stalls, and helped groom and feed them.

Briar was happiest in the stables or the paddock, her

boots caked with dirt and muck, hat on her head, treats in her coat pockets to win over the stubborn horses and reward the sweet ones. Soft words went so much further than harsh ones. Treats were better than punitive actions. The horses trusted her, even the most fearful.

If only she trusted herself.

If only she wasn't afraid, because she was. She was afraid that in three and a half months she'd be struggling with a baby, struggling to make ends meet. She didn't know the first thing about small humans. She'd always preferred dog sitting to babysitting. Yes, she'd had good parents herself, but that didn't mean she was meant to be a mom—not that fate cared.

Abortion hadn't been an option. She hadn't considered it for even two minutes. She just knew she couldn't do it, wouldn't do it, and it wasn't because of her dad, or the church, or God, or some politician sitting in a big office somewhere to tell her it was wrong. It wasn't right for her because it wasn't right for her. End of story.

Stopping in front of the cabin's front door, Briar noted the car to the left of the building, a little navy Subaru with snow tires, but Cade's truck was missing. Perhaps he was out on the property, or up at the big house. She knew he spent a lot of time with Miss Warner, the owner of the ranch.

Smashing the flurry of nerves, Briar used the bronze knocker on the door, a brisk *bang-bang* and waited. She couldn't hear any noise inside, and perhaps it was the thick logs, but it did seem awfully quiet. Briar stepped back and crossed to the window and peeked in. The kitchen was dark. She couldn't see any lights on in the rest of the house.

"They're not here," a deep male voice said behind her.

Briar turned quickly, caught off guard. She hadn't heard anyone approach and hadn't realized she'd been seen.

"Do you know where they are?" she asked, her gaze lifting and sweeping over the tall cowboy.

His taupe felt cowboy hat was pulled down low on his head, hiding his hair, but not the dark brown sideburns, the same dark brown as his eyebrows and lashes.

"Montana," he said, his eyes narrowing.

"Just came from there," she muttered, suddenly tired.

She wasn't as exhausted as she'd been a month ago, but she didn't have her usual energy. Hopefully she'd get it back soon.

He lifted a brow. "Sounds like you weren't expected."

"Great deduction, Sherlock."

Any warmth in his eyes faded, his square jaw hardening, expression flinty. "Seeing as you're not expected, or wanted, I'll give you exactly two minutes to hustle back to that broken-down truck of yours and get off the property—"

"Or what? Throw me off?" she interrupted with a laugh. "I don't think my brother would like that. Cade's a lot of things, but he's not abusive toward women."

The cowboy's eyes narrowed. He looked down at her for a long, silent, grim moment. "Briar Phillips," he said. "In person."

And the way he said it, it wasn't a compliment.

It wasn't nice at all.

"Cade's been talking," she said.

The cowboy shook his head. "No, actually. He's never mentioned you. Others have though. You're Pastor Phillips's kid."

His dismissive tone coupled with the word kid set her teeth on edge.

She rocked back in her boots, locked her knees, readying for a fight. "I'm twenty-two—"

"Good for you. All grown up and looking for trouble. Well, you've come to the wrong place. We don't need trouble here, not your kind of trouble—"

"What does that mean?"

He took a step toward her, closing the gap between them. His broad shoulders blocked the sun, and she had to tip her head back to see the features in his shadowed face.

"It means I know who you are, and the kind of trouble you like, and that's not needed here at the Sundowner Ranch. So, if you know what's good for you, I'd get in your truck and get out of here before it's dark and the roads ice up and you put you and that horse of yours in danger."

"And I thought Cade was an asshat."

The cowboy's light blue eyes searched hers for a long moment before he glanced down at his watch. "Two minutes," he said, "starting now."

Briar didn't know if she was amused or shocked, or a combination of both, but she laughed out loud, pretty much in his face. "I'm not going anywhere."

Cowboy didn't like it. His expression darkened further.

"With Cade gone, I'm in charge, and I haven't been given any instructions with regards to a runaway—"

"Not a runaway."

He glanced at his watch. "One minute and five seconds."

She met his gaze and smiled into his eyes, the smile that used to infuriate her former teachers and bosses, a smile that got her in detention and fired and worse. "You really think highly of yourself. Good for you. Confidence is important."

Then without waiting for a reply she crouched down to lift the heavy mat in front of the door, revealed the hidden key and picked it up. Briar flashed the key at him, and another smile, before unlocking the door and disappearing inside.

JET WATCHED HER disappear into Cade's cabin, heard the front door lock, dead bolt turning. Lights went on, a yellow glow coming from the kitchen.

He stood there for a moment furious. She was the last thing they needed here, the last thing *he* needed here. He'd come to the Sundowner Ranch to get away from the world and unnecessary problems and Briar Phillips was a big problem. Beautiful, alive, full of emotion and passion ...

everything he found attractive, but he didn't want to find her attractive, not when he knew her history, not when he knew her family.

He'd been to her father's Paradise Valley Cowboy Church a half dozen times over the years, and Jet respected her father's ministry, the work he did, the people he helped. He also knew that beautiful, headstrong Briar wasn't the proverbial good girl. She liked trouble and flaunted the rules simply to prove her independence.

Jet glanced at his watch, aware that Briar wasn't going to be able to stay in the cabin forever. She'd have to come out to deal with her horse, and he suspected she'd be out soon. But in the meantime, he wasn't sure what to do about Briar being here. There was a long-standing rule on the ranch that all visitors had to be checked in with Miss Warner, and he knew Briar had met Miss Warner in the past, but as Jet hadn't worked at the ranch when Cade's sister was here before, he wasn't sure if there should be a change in protocol.

Perhaps the best thing to do was send a message up to the big house and let Miss Warner know that Briar had arrived, and then he sent the same text to Cade, adding that Briar had let herself into Cade's house.

Jet was hoping Cade would then be the one to deal with his sister but moments later his phone rang, and it was Cade on the other end of the line. "Briar is there?"

"She arrived about fifteen minutes ago. She's got her horse with her, but it's still in the trailer."

"Put her on the phone."

"Can't. She's gone into your place and locked the door."

"You two have words?"

Jet grimaced. "There was something, not sure you'd call it words."

"Does Miss Warner know?" Cade asked.

"Just sent her a text. Is there something else I should do?"

"Yeah. Tell my sister to get up to the house and ask Miss Warner if it's okay if she stays. This is Miss Warner's property, and I want to make sure she's always comfortable."

"I can't imagine she'd have a problem with your sister being here."

"No, she won't, but it's courtesy. Miss Warner is old-school, and I respect that. I think everyone there understands that."

Jet cleared his throat. "You don't want to call your sister and tell her yourself?"

"You're in charge when I'm gone. You've got this. But if she gives you a hard time, you can send her packing. Tell her to come back when I return next week."

"Oh, she'd love that."

"Listen, I love my sister, but she's a bit of a hothead. If you really have a problem with her, let me know and I'll be happy to set her straight."

"Nah. I'm good. My mom wasn't exactly a hothead, but she was very independent. I can handle your sister."

"My mom was impulsive and troubled. Briar is so much

like her it makes me uncomfortable. I don't want her to end up like my mom."

"That's the situation," Jet said.

"Yes."

Hanging up, Jet walked past Briar's battered pale blue truck and silver horse trailer. The horse inside stomped a foot, indicating impatience with the situation. Jet looked into the trailer, and it wasn't a dainty mare inside, but a big chestnut gelding. The horse's ears went back and it gave Jet some serious side-eye. Jet shook his head. The horse had as much attitude as Briar. Thank goodness Cade would be back Sunday night to deal with both of them, because Jet didn't want to.

BRIAR MARCHED AROUND Cade's log cabin, knowing she needed to get back outside and deal with Judas, her horse, but dealing with Judas would mean she'd have to deal with that arrogant cowboy, and she was in no hurry to do that again.

Yes, he was big and muscular, with one of those chiseled faces so many women found handsome. She might have found him handsome if they'd met in different circumstances, but they hadn't, and now he was just plain annoying.

After sending a text to her dad to let him know she'd arrived at the Sundowner safely, Briar went into the kitchen, filled a glass with water, and drank it standing at the kitchen sink looking out the window. She was still there when the tall, muscular arrogant cowboy came into view. He was heading toward the cabin, and she started to shrink back when he stopped in front of the kitchen window and shouted at her through the glass. "Just talked to your brother. Cade said you're to head up to the big house and ask Miss Warner if it's okay for you to stay here a few days until he gets back."

Briar set her glass down. "Cade's not coming back for a few days?"

"He's spending the weekend with his Wyatt family outside Marietta."

Her stomach suddenly cramped, painful and heavy as if she'd swallowed a bucket of stones. She shouldn't be jealous that he had another family, people on his father's side, people that loved him and wanted him because obviously he deserved that as he hadn't had an easy childhood. But she wanted Cade to include her as family, and so far he didn't. But maybe she couldn't lay the blame at his door. She hadn't made things easy the last time she was here.

"So, once I talk to Miss Warner, I can stay?" she said.

"Instead of shouting through the window, why don't you open the front door?"

She rolled her eyes but went to the door and opened it. Cowboy was already there waiting for her with his dark hair, blue eyes, and square jaw with a hint of a shadow.

"You were the one who began talking to me through the

window," she said, all pins and needles and frustrated defiance.

He shrugged. "Easier talking to you through glass than thick wood."

"You have an answer for everything?"

"Do you like to fight about everything?" he countered.

She smashed her exasperation. "Should I drive the truck and trailer up to the house, or would it be better to walk up there?"

"I'll drive you. You ready now?"

She nodded. "Might as well get this over with."

After locking the door and slipping the key into her pocket, Briar walked alongside the cowboy to a glossy black truck, surprisingly shiny for being a ranch truck. "You must not drive this on the ranch too often."

"I was just in town yesterday. Thought I'd give it a wash before I went out."

"Have a date?"

"I did, not that it's any of your business."

He was right, of course, which made her bite her lip, effectively silencing her. But it didn't squash her curiosity. If anything, it made her want to ask more questions, which was odd as she didn't typically care what most men thought. Why he made her curious was beyond her. She didn't even know his name.

Which made her give him a long assessing look. "You have a name other than arrogant cowboy?"

He suddenly smiled, flashing her a look she couldn't define but it sent a frisson of sensation through her, making her feel even more sensitive.

"Some people call me Jet. Some people call me other names. But Jet is on my birth certificate."

"Jet what?"

"Jet Manning."

She looked at him and then out the window, brow furrowing. "Your name sounds familiar."

He didn't say anything, just started the truck and drove them up to the big house where five generations of Warners had been born and raised.

It was obvious he didn't want to talk to her but for some reason that just made her feel extra chatty. "You weren't here a year ago," she said.

"I was here a year ago," he corrected. "I started work February first." He glanced at her, his gaze unsmiling. "You apparently were here the month before me." He returned his focus to the rutted road lined with dirty snow. "Apparently the visit didn't go smoothly."

Briar's temper immediately spiked, and she counted to five to keep from saying something she might regret. "It was stressful," she conceded. "And emotional. For both of us."

"Never seen Cade emotional."

Briar pressed her fists to her thighs. "He wasn't weeping, no, but trying to catch up on our shared family history wasn't easy." She looked at him, equally unfriendly. "Are both of your parents still alive?"

"No." His single syllable answer was sharp and hard, discouraging further questions.

Even if she'd wanted to ask another question, they'd arrived at the Warners' house, a sprawling, soaring, log cabin home built in the park architecture style of the early 1900s. Park architecture swept North America, seeing the development of the elegant but rustic lodges dotting the new national parks. At night with the lights illuminating the big windows, the three-story house glowed, but in the middle of the afternoon it appeared dark and heavy and more than a little forbidding.

Jet shifted into park. "I'll walk you in," he said, "and then I'll wait for you outside. Whatever you do, be polite—"

"I am polite."

He arched a black eyebrow. "She's looking pretty frail right now, but she's all there mentally. Your brother is incredibly protective of her."

Briar nodded once, trying not to be offended. "I know."

BRIAR RANG THE doorbell and then stepped back and waited. Miss Warner's housekeeper Emma opened the door to Briar and waved her in. "We met before," she said. "I'm Emma, housekeeper and cook."

"Yes," Briar said, politely, and yet everything in her felt chilled and frustrated.

If only Cade was here. If only she could just deal with him; it would be so much better than this dog and pony show.

"I remember. It's nice to see you again. How is Willis?" she asked, referencing Emma's husband who managed the summer dude ranch program.

Emma closed the door behind Briar. "He's away at the moment, visiting family in San Diego, where the weather is much nicer. I'm trying not to be envious, but it's hard being left behind." But Emma was smiling and she didn't look that unhappy to be left behind. "Now Miss Warner is on the phone right now but once she's off she'll speak with you. Why don't you wait in the dining room and, as soon as she's off the call, I'll take you in?" Emma had walked Briar into the dining room and patted a chair near the end of the table.

Briar sat down feeling self-conscious. She could hear Miss Warner on the phone, and it sounded as if she was talking to Cade. Had she put him on speaker?

Emma seemed oblivious though. "Would you like anything? A cookie? Coffee? Cup of tea?"

Briar's stomach had been rumbling for the past hour, but she didn't want anyone fussing over her. "No, thank you. I'm fine."

"Well, if you change your mind, I'm right in the kitchen." She pointed toward a swinging door and then with a little pat on Briar's shoulder disappeared.

Alone in the dining room, Briar did her best to block out

Miss Warner's conversation, but she had the sound up and the voices carried.

"It's not a problem," Miss Warner was saying. "You'll be back in a few days, and we'll sort it all out. She's welcome to stay here, or if she's more comfortable in your house—"

"But I'm not comfortable with her there. She's just a stone's throw from the bunkhouse."

"I think you're worrying needlessly, Cade."

"Maybe, but what if you put her in the kitchen? Emma can use help."

"I get the feeling your sister is a horse woman, not a cook."

"Everyone needs to know how to cook. Food prep is part of life on the ranch. If she wants to stay here, my sister needs to work."

"I don't think she's going to be happy."

Cade made a short, impatient sound. "Dot, you and I both know that having her down amongst the ranch hands isn't going to work. She's pretty. And those boys don't see enough girls. We don't need them mixing, especially when I'm gone."

"I was pretty once, and I worked on the ranch, but that didn't mean I did the dirty with everyone, Cade—"

"It's Jet," Cade said, interrupting her. "I'm most concerned about Jet."

"Why Jet? He's the one I'd trust the most. He's not going to flirt with her!"

"Exactly. Which will drive Briar crazy. She's headstrong and can't resist a challenge. You and I both know Jet's not going to settle down, and he's not interested in a relationship. He's the kind of cowboy that takes what he wants, and makes commitments to no one, and I'm afraid my sister will find that virtually irresistible."

"You don't seem to think too highly of your sister, Cade."

"But I do. That's just it. I'm not there and I'm trying to protect her. I don't want Briar getting her heart stomped on by Jet. She hasn't had an easy life, or maybe it could have been easy, but she decided to make it hard—"

"Your sister is looking for a brother, Cade, not another daddy. From what I understand, she's got a good one, and she loves him."

Briar closed her eyes and pressed her knuckles to her forehead, embarrassed to hear how they were discussing her in such intimate detail. Thank goodness neither of them knew about her ... situation. She couldn't even imagine the conversation then.

"I just wish she'd told me she was coming. I would have asked her to wait a few days until Bee and I were home."

"She didn't know about your granddad's birthday, and it's fine with me. I have a big place here, lots of bedrooms, she'll be fine until you return."

For a moment, Cade didn't say anything and then he sighed. "I appreciate it, Dot. You know I do."

"Your family is my family. There's nothing to worry about. Worry just ages you."

"Yes, ma'am."

"So, who is going to tell her where she's staying and how she's going to be passing the time here?"

"I'll call her as soon as you're done talking to her."

"I'm happy to let her know I'd like her to stay here."

"And helping out? You'll let her know she's going to work with Emma?"

"Why don't you let her be a guest for a few days, Cade? Maybe she just needs a little vacation—"

"Then she shouldn't have come to the Sundowner. It's a working ranch this time of year. Summer is when we become the dude ranch."

"You sound a little grumpy, Cade. Everything okay?"

"Everything's fine. Just have a headache. Bee thinks I'm coming down with something. I just need a good night's sleep. I like coming to see Grandad and all, but these beds are little, especially when you add a baby and a pregnant wife."

"What about the portable crib?"

"Grace hates it, won't sleep in it, but it's alright. All is good. See you Sunday."

Briar heard the call end and started to stand and then sat back down. Her heart was racing, and she felt vaguely sick. She would have been far happier hearing none of that. It made her realize she still hadn't patched things up sufficiently with Cade.

Emma suddenly appeared in the dining room, wiping her hands on a yellow and white check dish towel. "Miss Warner's off her call. She's looking forward to talking with you."

Briar felt even more anxious now, but she forced a smile and murmured her thanks and walked numbly into the living room.

JET WATCHED BRIAR walk down the steps of Miss Warner's house back to his truck, long hair sliding over her shoulder, expression set, lips compressed. He couldn't tell from her expression if her meeting with Miss Warner had gone well or not, but she'd been in there for about ten minutes so some things had been said.

Briar opened the passenger door, and stepped up into the truck, closing the door firmly behind her.

He started the truck even as she sighed, a heavy sigh, and he glanced at her. "Everything okay?"

She nodded.

"You can stay?" he added.

She nodded again. Her lips pursed and she looked as if she was about to say something before thinking better of it.

"What?" Jet demanded. "Something's eating you."

"I have to stay up at the house." Briar looked out her window at the big log home. "She thought it was more appropriate seeing as Cade is gone."

Relief swept through him. For the first time since she'd arrived, he felt as if he could breathe. Briar belonged at Miss Warner's, not at Cade's, not so close to the bunkhouse full of testosterone-fueled males. "You won't be a prisoner there," he said.

"Yes, but Judas—"

"Judas?"

"My gelding."

Of course, Briar Phillips, rebel daughter of Pastor Patrick Phillips from Paradise Valley Cowboy Church would name her horse Judas. His lips almost curved. Almost. "Your horse will be fine in the barn. I imagine you probably want to get him settled before you head up to the house for the night."

"I really don't want to be at the house," she said, almost under her breath. "It's so ... fancy."

"Miss Warner likes her space. She won't be expecting you to entertain her all hours of the day."

"But dinner is at six, precisely, and I'm to wear something *nice*."

"She's not asking you to put on a cocktail dress."

"Good, because I don't own one."

He checked his smile as he accelerated, following the big circular driveway around, heading back the way they'd come. "Clean, dark denims will work with a nice blouse. Just don't show up in a T-shirt and work jeans."

"I'd rather stay at Cade's."

He didn't say anything because what could he say? Briar didn't like rules, structure, authority figures—the very things that made a big ranch run successfully.

"Can you please talk to her for me?" Briar asked, turning to face him, a pleading light in her eyes. "I'm happy to work while I'm here. I want to work. Put me to work—"

"Can't do that. Miss Warner wants you at the house. It's almost four now. That gives you a little over an hour to settle Judas and then head up to the house. Put your bags next to your truck and one of the hands will drive them up."

Her expression hardened. She looked away, muttered something unflattering, and then clammed up, which was just fine with Jet. The less said at this point the better.

Chapter Two

It took Briar almost an hour to settle Judas and then walk up to the house, hauling her luggage with her. She wasn't about to ask for a ride from anyone, and she had no desire to speak with Jet Manning, either. He was even colder and more caustic than Cade, which was saying a lot.

Emma opened the front door again and slowly took her up the stairs, and then down a long hall, and down another hall to a room with an enormous window that framed a spectacular winter sunset.

"Will this do?" Emma asked as she glanced around. "Haven't had guests here in a year or so, but it gets cleaned regularly."

"It's lovely," Briar said, "thank you. I'm sorry I'm making so much work for you."

"Not at all. I'm quite partial to Cade and it's very nice to have you here with us. Miss Warner will be glad for the company, too. Now, don't forget dinner is at six—"

"On the dot," Briar said.

"Just like Miss Warner's name," Emma said.

"Is Miss Warner's name Dot?"

"Well, Dorothy, yes, but her family always called her Dot, and Cade does, too."

"You don't?" Briar asked.

"Oh, no. I call her Miss Warner. But that's just how we've always been." Emma went to the door. "I'll see you downstairs at dinner."

The moment Emma was gone, Briar shut the door and then explored the room. The spacious bedroom had its own bathroom with a lovely sage-green marble, and it was really nice, definitely the nicest room she'd ever had with a little sitting area and a huge bed with elegant linens. The room was filled with antiques and what looked like very expensive framed oil paintings hung on the wall. The room was far more luxurious than Cade's old cabin, but she hadn't come to the Sundowner to be with Miss Warner. She'd come to work with the horses not the dishes.

She paced the room for a few minutes, trying to stay calm but her temper was getting the best of her. Unable to contain her frustration she grabbed her phone and punched in Cade's number. "It seems I came at the wrong time," she said.

"If you'd asked—"

"I know. I'm sorry." Tears filled her eyes. She was exhausted and stressed, and she'd been counting on Cade, needing his advice. "When will you be back?"

"Sunday."

It was only Wednesday. Sunday seemed far away. "Maybe I should go back home," she said. "I don't want to be in the way here."

"You won't be in the way if you help out," he said.

She drew a breath, seeing the opening she was looking for. "Is there any way I can work in the barn instead of the house?" She cleared her throat. "I came to work with the horses. That was my goal. Or at least on the property."

"The horses are in the east pasture now. It's their spring break and with Willis gone right now, it's best not to change things up. The horses are for the summer programs, and it's Emma that could use help," Cade said. "Willis used to handle some of the shopping and errands, so it'd be good if you could do that for her, along with assisting in the kitchen. It's a lot of work for her taking care of the house and prepping all the meals. It'd be good if you could help her out while you get the lay of the land."

"There is no land here in the house, Cade," she answered dryly. "You know I'm not very domestic. I feel trapped when I'm inside, like I can't breathe. I'm far more comfortable outside, on a horse. You have a dozen ranch hands here. Don't see why you can't use one more."

"Maybe," he said calmly, "if you can prove yourself to me."

"So, you are still mad at me."

"I'm not mad at you. But every single person at the Sundowner has had to earn my trust. You do, too."

"Even though I'm your sister?" Her voice quavered and

she closed her eyes, hating all the emotion rushing through her, making her feel as if she might crack and break. She was so tired and so worried, and it suddenly crossed her mind that this was not the right place to be. There would be no resting here.

"Don't take it personally, Briar. It's not personal."

She had to bite her tongue to protest but it was, that she'd overheard him talking to Miss Warner and he didn't want her around the other hands, that he was deliberately putting her in the kitchen. She was pretty sure no other ranch hand had to start in the kitchen. But saying any of this would only push him away, and Cade didn't like drama. She didn't want more tension between them. "Can I maybe do some work in the barn? Let me muck stalls. Move hay bales. Shovel gravel, snow ... just let me be outside—"

"The house is a good place for you, Briar. At least until I get back."

She blinked back tears. "I'm not interested in any of the guys here. I'm not looking for a boyfriend, not wanting to date—"

"Good, then you shouldn't mind being at the house. See you Sunday and try not to stir things up."

"Why do you say that?"

"Because you're feisty. You and I both know that. Good night, Briar. Be good to Miss Warner." He hung up without waiting for her to say goodbye.

Exhaling she glanced at her phone. Five forty. Twenty

minutes before dinner. Briar plugged in her phone, saw that she'd received a thumbs-up text from her dad, and turned her attention to unpacking her suitcase. So far, she'd been able to hide her pregnancy with vests and sweatshirts, oversized men's shirts raided from her dad's closet, but soon baggy clothes wouldn't be enough. She needed to share her news with her family. She just didn't know when or how.

After a hot shower, Briar dressed in dark denims and a long-sleeved Western blouse in a light brown leopard print which she topped with a pretty embroidered suede vest. The chocolate-colored vest was heavily fringed and covered her waist and middle. With her hair brushed, and wearing her best boots, she hoped she looked dressy enough for dinner. She didn't have a lot of fancy outfits. There was no reason for her to have evening or dressy clothes. She did have a few shorter skirts from the summer, including the short-fringed skirt she wore the night she met Garrett at Grey's Saloon, but it was too cold to wear those now, and with the amount of leg they showed, Briar didn't think they were appropriate for dinner.

Miss Warner gave Briar a warm smile when she appeared downstairs a few minutes later, and, as it was just the two of them for dinner, they went into the dining room and were seated, Briar's place mat and place setting to Miss Warner's right.

"That's usually where your brother sits," Miss Warner said. "At least when he joins me. Before he married, we had dinner every night. Now it's just on Sundays when MerriBee and little Grace join him." She sounded a little wistful. "Cade still has lunch with me once or twice a week, which I like. It's always nice to have time with him."

"Has it been a big change, him being married?"

"I see him every day. We talk every day, but it's not exactly the same as before, no. I am happy for him, though. He's a much happier person as well. He needed MerriBee and he just dotes on that baby. Grace has tied her daddy around her little finger already."

"Lucky little girl," Briar said.

Miss Warner gave her a long look. "Are you close with your dad?"

Briar hesitated. "I think I was when I was young, but it's been challenging these last ten years. I miss the relationship we had. To be honest, I'm not sure how to fix it."

"Why? What happened?"

Briar toyed with her spoon. "I rebelled a lot and I've lost his trust." She kept her gaze fixed on her plate. "But I'm determined to do better. I want to show him I'm more responsible now." *If it's not too late.*

"You talk as if you're in your thirties, not—" Miss Warner broke off, studied Briar, head tipped to the side. "Early twenties I think, yes?"

"Just had a birthday in February. I'm twenty-two."

"Twenty-two. You're still learning the important things, and that's good. We all make mistakes. It's what you do after the mistake that is important."

Emma entered the dining room to clear the dinner plates. "I have bread pudding tonight," she said, efficiently stacking plates and gathering cutlery, "with caramel sauce if you'd like. I can serve that now or in the living room while you watch TV?"

Miss Warner glanced at Briar. "Are you in a hurry to rush off, or would you like to join me for some television and dessert? I usually watch *Wheel of Fortune* and *Jeopardy* before I head upstairs. They're on rather early so Cade has set it up so they tape for me."

Briar hadn't grown up in a house that watched much TV, let alone game shows, but the idea of having dessert in front of the TV sounded fun. "I'd like to join you if you don't mind the company."

"I quite like your company so let's head to the other room." Miss Warner carefully pushed up and stood at the table for a moment making sure she had her balance. "And you want the bread pudding with caramel sauce. It's very good that way."

Briar looked at Emma and smiled. "Two for dessert then, but please don't bring it to us. Let me know when I should come in to the kitchen and I can get it."

"Then come in as soon as *Wheel of Fortune* finishes. It'll be ready then. Miss Warner likes dessert during *Jeopardy*."

"I'll do that. Thank you."

It was one of the nicest evenings Briar could remember

in a very long time. Miss Warner was sharp, and quite often knew the answers to the word puzzles before the contestants did. She'd comment on the prizes and shake her head when someone repeatedly lost a turn or went bankrupt. During commercials, if Miss Warner forgot to fast-forward through them, she'd mute them and talk to Briar about growing up with a father who was a pastor, and what it was like being on the road, hosting Sunday services during different rodeos.

"It was all I knew," Briar answered. "Dad would do the service, usually holding it early morning at the arena, and Mom would make coffee and have something for everyone to eat."

"How did she prepare the food if you were traveling? Did you have a trailer?"

"Yes. It was older but it worked. There were stalls for horses and then our living quarters."

"Your dad rides?"

Briar nodded. "He grew up in Oklahoma on a small cattle ranch, and competed on the rodeo circuit when he was younger, but when he got injured in his late twenties, he said it was because God had a different plan for him. He then went to Baylor University's Truett Seminary—he met Mom at Baylor. She was studying church music—and the rest is history."

"Love at first sight?"

"Pretty much," Briar agreed.

"Cade said your mom passed away when you were still in

school."

"I was fifteen."

"That had to be hard."

"It still is. I"—Briar took a quick painful breath—"miss her more now than ever. Everyone said it would get easier, but it hasn't." Her voice broke and she swallowed the rest of what she wanted to say. *I needed her. I still need her.*

Blinking, Briar noticed that the credits were rolling on *Wheel of Fortune*. They'd talked all through the end of the game. "I'll go get the bread pudding," she said, quickly rising, grateful to end the conversation.

˜

DOWN IN THE bunkhouse, it was even worse than Jet had expected. The ranch hands—all men in their twenties—sat down to the dinner table in high spirits. The discussion that night was all about the new arrival on the ranch, and whether Briar was single, and if she was indeed single, who had the best chances with her.

Jet let them talk, thinking eventually they'd run out of things to say. But no, the guys were happy to analyze everything about her, from her long dark hair to her stunning eyes. None of the others had gotten close enough to know the color, but Jet knew they were green, and she might be Cade's little sister, but she looked less like a cowgirl than a beauty queen. It wasn't just her face, either. She had long legs and a great butt, and when she walked, every guy in the vicinity stopped to check her out.

Yes, she was beautiful, but she was also barely out of her teens and the daughter of a minister, and Cade's little sister—three very strong reasons for him to keep his distance. But she wasn't just off-limits for him, she was off-limits for everyone, and he told the guys that when they couldn't move on to another subject.

"She's not available, so don't go there," Jet said flatly, wanting to squash the interest. "If you value your job here, you will steer clear. Cade will kill the guy that touches her. And I'm not kidding, either."

"He doesn't want *you* hooking up with her," Ace, one of the newer hands, said, grinning at Jet. "Because you're too old for her."

The eight men seated around the simple pine table laughed, with more than one glancing at Jet to see how he'd respond, but Jet ignored the laughter. He wasn't bothered by teasing, and he was used to having his authority tested. He'd joined the Navy after graduating from college, becoming part of the Navy's elite flight school, excelling in the rigorous program. But his mom's death in his late twenties changed him, knocking him off his career path. It had been four years since he'd left active duty, but it was hard to take the training out of the man.

The Navy had taught him what was important and what wasn't. Respecting authority was important. Getting caught up in drama wasn't.

While the younger guys cleaned up, Jet returned to the barn to check on the horses one last time. It was going to be another windy night and he wanted to be sure the doors were secure—last night one of them had blown open—and that couldn't happen again. But reaching the barn he discovered that while the night lights were on, the inside of the barn glowed with light, too.

He heard a voice coming from a back stall. A woman's voice pitched low, crooning words he couldn't understand but knew immediately it was Briar with Judas. As he walked down the aisle, several of the horses stuck their heads out to see where he was going. His horse nickered at him, and he gave a pat as he passed by.

"Hello?" Briar called out, sticking her head around the wall.

"It's me," Jet answered. "Just doing my final lockup."

"I can take care of that if you tell me what to do," Briar said, stepping out of the stall.

"That's alright. I'm not in a hurry. Take your time."

Judas put his head over the wall and Briar fed him a piece of a carrot from her pocket. "I wish I could sleep in here," she said, giving Judas another bit of carrot.

"What's wrong with your room at the house?" Jet asked, leaning against a column, arms folded over his chest.

"Nothing. It's just ... really nice. *Too* nice. I'm not used to that kind of luxury. A trailer or even some fresh, loose hay and a horse blanket suits me better."

"You might like it out here in summer, but it's going to get cold tonight."

She looked past him to the entrance of the barn. "Listen to the wind. It's got a lot to say."

He tipped his head, intrigued despite himself. "What is the wind saying?"

She turned her head and listened, giving him her striking profile with the long lashes, straight nose, and lovely lips. He couldn't look away from her face, drawn to her despite his best intentions.

"I don't know what you hear," she said thoughtfully, "but to me, it sounds like a mother calling her children." She glanced at him, still serious. "It just sounds so mournful."

She was smart, he realized, and there was more to her than met the eye. Probably being so pretty worked to her disadvantage. People probably expected her to be fluffy or silly, or worse, unkind.

"I have quite the imagination," she added, lips curving. "I've heard that my whole life."

His mother used to say the same thing, *I have quite the imagination*, and she'd say it the same way Briar did, with pride and more than a little bit of defiance. His mother had been a young mother, just sixteen when she had him, and until he finished college, it had been the two of them against the world. Joining the Navy meant he had to move away, but he hadn't abandoned her. He would never do that.

"Imagination's a good thing," he said, voice clipped, because thoughts of his mother inevitably created pain and he was ready to move on to something less uncomfortable. "Are you all set for tomorrow? You know where to be, and what to do?"

Briar nodded. "I'm free until ten when I report to the kitchen. Emma is going to teach me how to cook." She smiled ruefully. "I'm supposed to be there to help her, but I don't think Miss Warner and Cade understand that I'm going to just get in Emma's way."

Jet pushed off the column and walked toward Judas's stall. The horse eyed him warily but by the end of the week Jet knew Judas would settle in. Jet wasn't so sure about Briar, but he kept that to himself. "Emma's missing Willis who has been gone for a couple of weeks now. She'll be glad to have your company. Without Willis here, she doesn't have anyone to fuss over."

"What about Miss Warner?" Briar asked, looking at him, her long dark hair sliding over a shoulder.

"Miss Warner doesn't like too much attention. The secret to getting along with her is letting her have control. She'll talk to you when she wants to talk to you, and when she wants to be left to her thoughts, she won't engage you."

"Then maybe I should give you some pointers for Judas," Briar said, snapping what was left of her carrot into two pieces and giving Jet both. "Judas likes compliments and treats. So, if you want him to tolerate you, you'll need to be patient and spoil him. A lot." She gave Jet a somewhat mocking smile and walked out of the barn.

Jet heard her close the big barn door behind her, the latch securing and then turned to look at Judas who was eying him.

"Compliments and treats, is it?" Jet said, opening his hand so that Judas could take one of the carrot pieces.

Judas hesitated only for a moment before taking it. He promptly looked at Jet for more. Jet gave him the last piece but only after making the handsome gelding endure a pat or two.

※

BACK IN HER room, Briar couldn't sleep. After being outside, her room was too warm, too formal, too everything for her comfort. She wasn't accustomed to big four-poster beds with fluffy duvets and equally thick, fluffy feather mattress toppers. All the softness seemed to swallow her up, and she turned this way and that, hot, miserable, trapped.

If she wasn't pregnant, she wouldn't even be here.

If she wasn't such a fool…

Why hadn't she insisted Garrett wear a condom? What had happened to her brain? Why didn't she believe you could really get pregnant on your first time?

Her stupidity still blew her mind.

Briar left the bed and walked to the window overlooking the land with the mountains and valleys. The heavy clouds cloaked the mountains tonight, but she knew they were there. She could feel them, feel the weight of the land and the history. In some ways, it wasn't so different from Montana, but in others, it was completely different. She didn't belong here, and yet, she did. If Suzy, her birth mother, had kept her, she would have been raised in Story, Wyoming, not far from here. If Suzy had raised her, would she have suffered as Cade had? Or would things have been different? Would *she* have been different? Less wild and rebellious? Or, a new thought struck, even more troubled? Briar shuddered, unable to imagine it.

She couldn't blame her situation on her upbringing. She'd been raised in the church, raised to know right from wrong. So why had she fallen for Garrett? Why did she think he was the one? Not the one for marriage, but the one to be her first?

It was such a bad decision. He didn't love her, and as it turned out, barely liked her, and in the end, the whole experience was actually rather dreadful. Virginity lost, Garrett had won and was done, and there was no one she could talk to about it. Who did the daughter of a pastor confide in?

Certainly not her dad. He'd just be hurt and oh so disappointed. The disappointment would kill her. She'd already let him down in so many ways. He deserved better. He deserved a daughter more worthy of his patience and love.

Her eyes prickled and burned, and she sat down in the chair near the window and took the soft fuzzy blanket from the arm of the chair and wrapped it around her shoulders to keep warm.

It didn't seem fair that terrible sex could result in a baby. Honestly, one should have to have an orgasm for a baby. *Some* kind of pleasure. The whole thing had been awkward and uncomfortable and rushed and then it was over, leaving her feeling empty and ashamed.

Turned out being wild and rebellious wasn't as exciting as she'd thought.

Being wild and rebellious hadn't been worth it.

Talk about a come-to-Jesus moment, but in this case, Jesus couldn't help her. No one could help her. Only Briar could decide if she was going to keep the baby or give the baby up. That was the struggle. That was why she was here. She needed to talk to Cade. She needed someone she trusted to talk it through with her.

Right now, her head told her that adoption made the most sense. Her head told her she was young and there would be opportunities for children when she was mature and married.

Her head told her she was completely financially dependent on others, which meant living at home with her dad, or possibly living here where Cade worked.

But she couldn't be at home with her dad, not while she grew bigger and bigger, the evidence of her irresponsibility on full display. Her dad shouldn't have to help her raise a child. Not because he wouldn't be a good grandfather, as he most certainly would be a most devoted grandparent, but her dad would silently, privately grieve for her. He'd grieve for the loss of possibilities, grieve that instead of reaching for her dreams and pursuing her passions, she'd had to shift her focus to becoming a young mother.

Briar had seen young mothers out with their babies. She'd seen them at the malls and fast-food restaurants. She'd seen them pushing strollers and balancing babies on their lean girlish hips. Briar had never envied them, not for a moment. She valued her freedom too much. She couldn't imagine having to take care of a little human twenty-four seven. Good gracious, she could hardly take care of herself.

She had terrible self-loathing and almost no self-worth.

She hated herself for everything she'd put her parents through, hated herself for her selfishness, and her inability to yield and just be the daughter they wanted.

Their dream daughter would lead a young-adult Bible study, their dream daughter would help with Sunday services and take time off her schedule to go see those in need of TLC and prayer. But Briar wasn't a minister, and she didn't feel called to serve, not in that capacity. She wasn't sure what she believed. She just knew she was nothing like her parents and it all made sense when she found out she wasn't theirs, not biologically.

Of course, she wasn't like them. She wasn't their DNA. She was the product of some married woman named Suzy having an affair, and then forced to give the newborn up because her violent drunk husband wouldn't let her bring the baby home.

Briar's eyes stung. No wonder she was a mess from conception. She'd been conceived in sin.

❦

EVEN THOUGH SHE slept poorly, Briar was up early, waking at five just as she did at home. Just as she did at home, she dressed warmly and headed downstairs to the kitchen where she filled her water bottle and quietly let herself out of the house.

It was dark outside, and the morning was cold, a little over forty degrees but according to the weather report on her phone, it would warm up to high fifties later. Thankful for her soft fluffy parka and thick fur-lined gloves, she drew up short when she spotted Jet in his horse's stall. "Did you sleep in here last night?" she said, lifting a brow.

"No, but I should have. The bunkhouse isn't the best place to get a good sleep. It's gassy and loud."

"Guys up late talking?"

"No. Guys asleep snoring."

She couldn't help smiling. "That does sound terrible. Maybe I won't complain about my big bed with the Egyptian cotton sheets."

"That's probably a good idea," he said, putting a halter on his horse and leading him out of the stall. "By the way, I wasn't sure if you were hoping to ride early, so I fed Judas for you. If that was a mistake just let me know and I won't do it again."

"That was nice of you," she said, her surprise evident in her voice.

"I can be," he answered, tone dry. "Do you remember the lay of the land? Don't want to annoy you with mansplaining."

"Are you in the habit of mansplaining?" she answered, trying not to laugh.

Having woken up in a troubled mood, Briar didn't think anything could lift her spirits, but Jet, with his reference to the gassy, noisy bunkhouse and his determination not to be condescending was making her smile. Perhaps the gorgeous high-handed cowboy wasn't quite as awful as she'd thought. Maybe just seventy percent awful, if she could apply a percentage to his arrogance.

"No, but then again, we don't usually have any young women here."

"And you wouldn't dream of being condescending to Miss Warner or Emma."

"Absolutely not. My days would be numbered here."

She darted a glance in his direction, trying to read his expression. "You like it here?"

"It's become home," he answered leading his horse away, but then stopped, and pointed to the tack room. "You'll find all your gear in there. We like to keep everything pristine in case Miss Warner wanders down."

"Does she still ride?"

"She hasn't since summer, but she still keeps three horses—"

"Three?"

"She's a horsewoman, and her horses are her family."

"I thought Cade was her family."

Jet shot her a curious look. "Are you jealous of Miss Warner?"

Briar immediately wished she'd said nothing. She had a tendency to say the first thing that came to mind, and it was not a strength. The sooner she learned to be less impulsive the better for all. "Not jealous of her, but I wish I knew Cade better. I wish I felt closer to him."

"Is that why you're here now? You've come here to spend time with him."

"I worry that if it doesn't happen soon, it will never happen. I waited years to find him but when we met it was … awkward. It felt stilted and even after a few days we still didn't know how to talk to each other."

"Then it's good you're here. MerriBee works hard and with the baby they're both busy. I'm sure MerriBee would love help with Grace—"

"I don't want to be a babysitter," Briar said swiftly, cutting him short. "But I'm happy to help out in other ways. Hopefully working with the horses. I'm a good trainer. It's what I've done since high school. I'd like to have my own stable one day. That's really my goal."

"Well then, let me let you focus on Judas before you have to be at the house." He nodded at her and walked his horse to where his tack waited for him.

As Briar brushed Judas, she watched Jet from the corner of her eye as he placed the pad on his horse's back and then added the saddle. He was confident, she thought, and very comfortable in his skin, unlike the young guys who were always trying to prove something to someone. Like Garrett.

Suddenly two young cowboys entered the barn and stopped to talk to Jet. She saw them glance her way, and then Jet must have said something to them about her, because they grinned and shook their heads, even as they looked over at her again. She looked back at them, chin up, not sure why the young cowboys were smiling but not about to be cowed, either.

If she'd learned anything these past six months, it was to avoid the opposite sex. Men like Garrett had made her realize how easy it was for them to say sweet things and make promises they never intended to keep.

No, Briar was done with guys, so Cade didn't have to worry about her there. She wasn't interested in any of his young cowboys—she glanced at Jet and discovered he was looking at her, but he wasn't smiling—and, grinding her teeth together, knew she most definitely wouldn't make a move on him, either.

Suddenly, she didn't feel much like riding or being in the barn. Briar finished grooming Judas and, after returning the brush and comb, she walked up to the house, frustrated and confused. She felt angry but angry at whom? Herself? Garrett? Everyone? Shaking her head, Briar stepped into the house as the first streak of light appeared over the mountains.

BRIAR'S FIRST DAY in the kitchen at the Warner house wasn't awful, but it was long. She wasn't used to chopping a mountain of vegetables into itty bitty pieces. She was slow and awkward, and every time Emma took a knife and gave her a little tip to improve her technique, Briar felt more useless than ever.

"We're making a big pot of soup," Emma said. "Beef barley, and then we're going to get a head start on tonight's chicken enchiladas. I like to season and roast the chicken breasts early in the day so they've cooled and are easy to shred for when we roll up the enchiladas later."

Briar nodded, doing everything she was told but finding it hard to be as passionate about meal prep as Emma. To Briar's thinking, food was food and for her, a little went a long way. Only she couldn't say any of that to Emma. She couldn't say that to anyone. Briar didn't have any close friends, having pushed her high school crowd away after she graduated. There weren't that many, either, as the group she hung out with thought that it was really weird her dad was a pastor.

Briar used her hand to slide all the chopped onions, carrots, and celery into the big stainless-steel bowl. "Now what?" she asked, smiling, determined to be cheerful. Determined to be grateful. Determined to be the Briar her mother had raised her to be.

"Could you get the chicken breasts out of the refrigerator? We will want all the packages in there," Emma said.

It was a *lot* of chicken. Briar set the two huge packages on the counter and wrinkled her nose, a little grossed out by so much raw poultry, the skinless breasts so shiny.

"I will have you season those." Emma pointed to the cupboards. "Chile powder, cumin, garlic powder, onion powder, salt and pepper, and maybe a little oregano."

Briar unwrapped the chicken and stared at the eight fleshy breasts. "Do I mix the seasoning together first, and how much of each?"

"Dab the breasts to dry them and then place them on the roasting pan over on the stove, and then sprinkle the seasonings on." Emma gestured with her hand as if sprinkling seasoning was in every woman's repertoire. "Oh, and paprika. Don't forget the paprika."

Briar did as she was told, holding her breath, expecting Emma to correct her at any moment but Emma just left her to it. She sprinkled and sprinkled and once finished, looked at Emma.

Emma nodded her approval. "Now just a drizzle of olive oil. I could have had you do it first, but I don't think it matters. After you're done, slide the tray in the oven and it will cook for forty-five minutes or so."

"Why so much chicken?" Briar asked, completing that task. "It's like we're feeding an army."

"We are. Well, not an army, but all of the ranch hands."

"They don't cook their own meals?" Briar asked, washing her hands thoroughly.

"They do a couple days a week, but it's easier for everyone if I just feed them all at the same time."

Briar dried her hands. "And who does all the dishes?"

"The boys do theirs and I do ours." Emma gave Briar a smile. "Your brother said you would be doing the dishes while you were here, but I'm not going to hand over all of my jobs. What would I do? Paint my nails?"

Briar glanced at Emma's hands with the short-clipped nails and only the one ring, her wedding ring. "Do you make everyone the same thing?"

"Generally. The boys just get a lot more." Emma set down her knife and went to one of the double ovens and peeked inside. The scent of lemon wafted out. "The cake's almost done." She closed the door and rinsed her hands. "Now we start on lunch."

Briar desperately held on to her smile. *Cheerful,* she told herself, *be cheerful, you're here to help.* And yet underneath the bright smile she couldn't believe they weren't even halfway through the day yet. What had she gotten herself into, coming to the Sundowner Ranch?

Chapter Three

B RIAR DIDN'T SEE Jet for the next two days. She avoided going to the barn when she thought he might be around, and convinced herself that she was happy being in the kitchen with Emma. Briar discovered she was genuinely content spending her evenings with Miss Warner watching television game shows.

It had been years since Briar had spent a significant amount of time with women, whether it was older women or girls her age. In those years, she'd convinced herself that she didn't need friends and didn't need guidance or acceptance or whatever it was women offered each other.

But after a few days, Briar conceded that both Emma and Miss Warner were good company, and genuinely tried to make her feel welcome and comfortable, and in return, Briar wanted to make things easier for both of them.

Briar began taking over the evening dishes so Emma could get off her feet earlier, and Miss Warner ended up waiting to start her evening programs until Briar joined her. When Briar said she didn't want Miss Warner to have to wait, Miss Warner said she'd rather watch them with Briar than watch alone because Briar often came up with good answers.

"You and Miss Warner seem to be getting along really well," Emma said the next morning when Briar showed up in the kitchen.

"I love her stories. She's fascinating. I can see why Cade cares about her so much. She's really special." Briar washed her hands well and dried them on a clean dish towel. "What would you like me to do first?"

"Mix up that spice rub and then we'll get the pork shoulder in it."

Briar glanced down at the recipe. "Pulled pork?"

"The guys love it. It's Cade's favorite and he'll be back tomorrow."

Briar frowned. "Is it Saturday already?"

Emma nodded. "The last few days flew by. I've enjoyed having you help me. Makes the day pass much more quickly."

"I'm not that much help," Briar answered, gathering the dry seasonings from the spice cabinet. "If anything, I slow you down and get in your way."

"But I like the company. I like *your* company." Emma gave Briar a quick hug. "I sometimes think that if I'd had children, they'd be right about your age now."

Briar had just started to measure the paprika into a small bowl and glanced up at Emma. "You never had kids?"

Emma flipped the dough on the floured breadboard.

"No. We weren't blessed with any."

"But you wanted them?"

"Oh, yes. Willis was one of nine kids and couldn't wait to start a family. I was an only child and really wanted to have kids, two, three, four, but it didn't happen. Years passed and we consulted doctors, but they couldn't explain it. It was just—not in God's plan."

It felt like a weight was resting on Briar's chest, making it hard to breathe. "Did you consider adoption?"

Emma expertly rolled the dough into a large thin circle. "We talked about it, yes, we did. We even went through an interview and then a home meeting with an agency, but they didn't like that we didn't have a house of our own, that we live here on the ranch."

Briar put the garlic powder down. "Why would that be an issue? I'd think growing up here on the Sundowner would be a wonderful thing for a child."

"I'm not totally sure. In hindsight, I think it wasn't normal enough. Miss Warner offered us a place of our own, said she'd even have a house built but the agency wasn't comfortable. I'm not sure if it's because we're too isolated here or with the ranch hands there were too many adult males in close proximity, but it was a no, and after that, we just couldn't do it anymore. Willis took it very badly and I was so disappointed, but I couldn't let him know how upset I was, or he would just feel worse." She looked up and managed a smile. "But we got through it and we're happy. We love working here, and we get to spoil Grace. We're honorary grandparents."

Briar didn't feel much better. Emma would have been such a good mom and there were so many children in the foster care system that could have used Emma's warmth and patience. Excused until four thirty, Briar walked down to the barn to see Judas but the entire time she groomed him, her thoughts were focused on what Emma had shared with her.

If Emma and Willis had wanted a baby that bad, there had to be others with similar stories, countless others who craved a child and dreamed of having a family when they couldn't have a baby themselves.

Briar thought of her parents who hadn't ever been able to conceive, and the letter Suzy, her biological mother, had written to her saying she'd chosen the Phillips because they'd longed for a family, they longed for a child.

If Briar gave up her baby, she could make someone very happy. She could fulfill a couple's dream.

LATER THAT AFTERNOON Briar learned that Cade and his family wouldn't be returning Sunday after all. Everyone knew before Briar, too. Cade phoned Miss Warner first and broke the news, and then called Jet who had been left in charge during Cade's absence.

"Grace is sick," Cade explained. "It's a pretty hard-core stomach thing. I'm not feeling great, trying to fight it.

There's no way we're going to make it back in the morning. Hoping by Monday or Tuesday we'll be on the road."

Jet opened the door of the bunkhouse and stepped outside. "How's MerriBee holding up?"

"Still healthy, but she's doing the majority of the caretaking, so I don't know how she'll avoid it, especially as Bee is the only person Grace wants right now."

"Hopefully MerriBee is masking up and washing her hands."

"Pretty much nonstop," Cade agreed. "I don't want to get this thing. It's not fun."

"Stay put if you can. We're all doing fine here. Don't push to return if you're not well. It's a long drive when you're healthy, never mind sick."

"Yeah." Cade hesitated. "What about Briar? How is she doing?"

"You haven't talked to her lately?"

"No. Why?"

"I don't know. She's your sister."

"She's not causing problems?"

"No. She's doing really well. Miss Warner likes having her here, too. She has Briar join her in the evenings to watch TV and have dessert."

"That's what I used to do."

"Before you got married and abandoned her."

"That's not what happened," Cade protested.

Jet laughed. "I know. I'm just giving you grief."

"Don't. I feel terrible. Praying I don't start throwing up. I hate throwing up."

"Get some ginger. That always helps me."

"Bee is already forcing me to drink ginger tea. It's disgusting." Cade sighed. "I just feel bad leaving you in charge this long. I thought I'd only be away five days."

"Tomorrow it will be five days. Unfortunately, your plans have changed but I've had a lot more responsibility than this in my life. This is easy."

"I know you're competent, but with Willis and me gone at the same time—"

"Everything here is fine. Briar is actually a very hard worker. When she's not in the kitchen she's spending time with Judas—"

"Judas?" Cade interrupted.

"Her horse."

"Of course."

Jet smiled. "I said the same thing."

"Her dad is a pastor."

"I know but I'm beginning to think she's not really a true hellraiser. Underneath her tough exterior, she's rather sweet. However, it's your ranch and once you're back you can decide what you want to do with her, and if you even want her on the ranch long term."

"Do you think she wants to stay?"

"I get the feeling she's looking for a new start."

"I wonder why." But then, before Jet could answer Cade

groaned. "Oh, no. I have to go. I'll be in touch later."

MISS WARNER INVITED Jet to join them for Saturday night dinner which baffled Briar. Why was Miss Warner including Jet when Cade had said he wanted to keep Briar up at the house away from the ranch hands? But then, during dinner Miss Warner spent most of the meal discussing an article she'd recently read in the *Wyoming Livestock Roundup* with Jet. She couldn't remember if the Sundowner was a member of the Wyoming Hay and Forage Association, a nonprofit devoted to promoting the hay and forage industry in the state, and when Jet answered he believed they were, because he and Cade had met with the director of the association last summer at the Wyoming State Fair, that pleased Miss Warner.

"We only raise enough hay here to take care of our livestock," Miss Warner said, "and there are years where we have to supplement from other ranchers and I keep thinking it's a mistake to buy from elsewhere when we could be doing it ourselves, saving money and creating another revenue stream."

"The altitude of the Sundowner Ranch requires you to invest a lot of money into improving your soil, but there are years where even best practices in fertilizers and irrigation don't pay off, especially with the droughts. When you compare the yield to profit, it's a wash. Sometimes even a loss," Jet answered.

"So, you're familiar with growing hay."

"It's one of the things Cade has asked me to focus on. I've been happy to learn what I can."

"If it was your money, what would you do?"

"I'd invest in a farm in Johnson or Sheridan County and concentrate on just alfalfa. As you know you can get a third-cut hay there whereas up at our elevation we're lucky to have two."

Briar left them talking at the table while she cleared the plates and then washed the dishes. It was interesting listening to the discussion as she'd never thought about where hay came from or who was growing it. Her dad always bought his alfalfa from the Marietta feed store and had it delivered to their barn. Of course, she'd read in newspapers about droughts and hay shortages in the past, but it hadn't been her problem and she'd let it go right over her head.

But being on the ranch, and listening to discussions like this, made her respect ranchers and growers all over again. They depended on weather—something they couldn't control—and yet the sun, rain, and daily temperature all impacted their livelihood.

Jet entered the kitchen then, carrying the water glasses and a few forgotten utensils.

"Thank you," Briar said, taking them from him and adding them to the hot sudsy water. She'd expected him to leave then but he picked up a towel and started drying the plates.

"You don't need to do that. You have enough work here on the ranch."

"I don't mind," he answered. "I'm not afraid of work. It's something I've always done, and something I would always do."

"Where did you get your work ethic from? Dad or Mom, or both?"

"Mom," he said rather shortly.

Briar wondered if she'd said something wrong and wasn't sure how to proceed but was saved from further awkwardness by the appearance of one of the ranch hands.

"Hey, sorry to barge in like this," the tall, skinny cowboy said, blushing a little as he nodded at Briar. "But some of us are going out tonight and we wondered if you'd want to come."

Briar wasn't sure if the blushing cowboy was talking to her or Jet, and she looked at Jet to gauge his expression.

"I'm in tonight," Jet said. "Thanks for checking in, though."

The lanky cowboy turned to Briar, blushing even more furiously. "What about you, Miss Phillips? We're going to go dancing. You're welcome to come."

Briar shook her head quickly. "I can't. I have to be up early. But thank you for the invitation, that's very kind of you." She hesitated. "What is your name?"

"Rolly Bertram," he said.

She smiled at him. "I've never met a Rolly before."

"It's actually Roland, but no one has ever called me that."

Jet cleared his throat and made a show of hanging up the dish towel. "If you're good here, I'll walk Rolly back to the bunkhouse."

Briar nodded, her gaze briefly meeting Jet's. There was heat in his eyes, and she wasn't sure if it was a warning or danger. Briar looked away, feeling scorched.

She didn't understand it, but then, she didn't understand him.

BRIAR WAS RELIEVED there was no Jet up at the house Sunday morning. After breakfast she headed up to her room and paced the floor a few times feeling restless. She wanted to do something, but Sunday was the one day everyone had off at the Sundowner, and she didn't want to bump into Jet, or the other ranch hands. She was happy then when just a few minutes later she saw trucks departing from near the barn, including Jet's black truck. It looked as if all the hands were heading into town, or at least, those who hadn't gone out drinking and dancing the night before.

With Jet gone, Briar changed and headed to the barn to take Judas out. The sky was clear, and the day wasn't warm, but it wasn't cold either, making it perfect for a long ride. But even as she reached the barn, she felt a good hard kick in her side and she froze, surprised by the strength of the kick.

Briar put a hand to her belly and there was another immediate kick.

Briar laughed and rubbed the spot. "You certainly have attitude," she said, before continuing on.

Yet once she was in the barn and grooming Judas she thought of that vigorous kick and for the first time she wondered if it was still safe to ride in her third trimester. She was so fit, and secure in the saddle, that she hadn't really thought it necessary to stop riding but now she wasn't sure what was recommended.

Instead of saddling Judas, she took him out and did some long-rein training with him which exercised him but kept her safely on the ground. Later, she'd look up more information but for now she felt good about her decision. With just three months to go, there was no point in taking unnecessary risks.

JET STOOD JUST inside the barn watching Briar work with Judas. She wasn't kidding when she said she liked training horses. She was also very skillful, far more knowledgeable than many cowboys twice her age. He was just leaving the barn when she walked Judas back in, and she drew up short as if shocked to see him.

"When did you get back?" she asked, reaching up to pat Judas's neck.

"I didn't go anywhere."

She frowned. "But I saw your truck leave earlier, when the others left."

"I loaned my truck to Brent. He wanted to go see his girl, but he doesn't have a car at the moment. He usually hitches a ride with one of the guys."

"That was nice of you," she said, changing hands on the lead. "Hope he brings it back in one piece."

"He should. Brent is on his way to take his girl to church."

"Good for Brent. My dad would approve."

Jet lifted a brow at her tone. "But not you?"

"I believe," she answered, "but do I have my father's faith? No. Not at all. He's aware of how I feel, too, and he doesn't judge me. He's of the mind that he will just love me to the Lord." Her lips quirked but there were shadows in her eyes, a tangible sadness that made him want to ask more questions, but that wouldn't help either of them. He'd vowed to keep his distance from her, and he fully intended to honor that vow even though he felt the pull between them, an intriguing awareness that was oh, so dangerous.

"I like your dad," Jet said simply.

"I do, too." She flashed him that slightly sardonic smile of hers and continued on into the barn.

Jet watched her, her butt rounded, her hips curved, her stride long. She was beautiful, graceful, athletic, strong.

And vulnerable.

He didn't know what her story was, but she most definitely had one, and he sensed it wasn't happy. She wasn't happy. There was something going on with her, something in her life that brought her to the Sundowner. Did she really need her brother, or was she just looking for a place to camp out?

Who—or what—was she avoiding?

Who—or what—had driven her here?

Normally, Jet didn't care about puzzles. He wasn't interested in human dramas. But for some reason Briar was different. He liked her, responded to her, and even though he was physically drawn to her, there was something beyond the physical drawing him to her, and perhaps that was the most baffling thing of all.

He didn't feel emotions, not anymore.

It was confusing to the women in his life, but Jet was fine being cold and hard, and emotionally out of touch. At least those were the things women hurled at him as they gathered their clothes and left his bed. Or as he gathered his clothes and left theirs.

It wasn't as if he couldn't feel at all, but he preferred not to. He avoided attachments. He knew how to pleasure in bed. And that was what he brought to a relationship. Sex. Really good sex, but sex without strings, sex without emotions, sex without a future.

He hadn't been an unfeeling son of a bitch his entire life, but he was comfortable now with the label, glad to be labeled ruthless and insensitive, as when he did care, he cared deeply, and felt strongly. The intensity of those feelings had got him in trouble in the past, which was why he learned to tamp it down, containing needs and wants until they were nearly nonexistent.

Yet another reason why he lay down the ground rules early. Sex was great. Hanging out was fine. But there would be no commitments. He wasn't going to get serious. He wasn't looking for a wife. He couldn't ever imagine falling in love and kids weren't ever part of the plan.

It wasn't that he disliked children, but there was no point in creating a family when he was rootless. He couldn't picture himself ever settling down and living in one place. He'd never spent more than a few years in the same place, and he wouldn't be at the Sundowner much longer, maybe six more months, maybe a year. But this desperado life of his wasn't a fair thing to do to a child, pull them away from the familiar world, over and over.

He wasn't criticizing his mother or his own childhood. It was just an observation as his mom was the kindest, most selfless human being he'd ever known, but even for her, parenting was hard. She'd apologized to him time and again for not providing better, for not having the resources to give him what he needed. She hated the struggles, which meant they were always moving around, in and out of different apartments, and then there was that one hard summer where they lived in her car, until the car got towed and his mom couldn't afford to get it back. But despite their struggles, and the moves and the lack of financial security, his mother had been loving. She'd smile often, always full of hugs and dreams and plans.

One day they'd own a beautiful house.

One day she'd buy him a car.

One day she'd go back to school and get a college education.

One day they'd visit the Kennedy Space Center in Florida.

One day Jet might even be an astronaut—if he studied hard and did well in school.

His mom, Katie, knew a lot about stars and was forever looking up at the sky pointing out constellations. She taught him to love the night sky and the peacefulness of the world when everything was dark and the city had gone to sleep. They'd sit together at the window and just take it in. No words were necessary. The universe was vast and full of possibility.

Jet had loved her unreservedly, and when he was young, he still had the ability to feel and love. He had girlfriends in high school and there was one he thought was special, maybe they'd marry after he went to college and had a job, but then her family left Butte for Houston. Then in May of his junior year, his mom lost her job and they decided to leave Butte, too, starting fresh in Polson, a charming little town on the southern tip of Flathead Lake.

Jet excelled at Polson High, but then he'd always been an

outstanding student and a gifted athlete. He was well liked, not because he was the life of the party, but he was tall, strong, and confident. His mother used to tease him that he had the face of an angel—it wasn't true—but girls were drawn to him and guys respected him and he took it all in stride. He wasn't wanting to be popular. He wanted to be successful and provide for his mom so she didn't have to work so hard, and she could one day have that house she dreamed of.

Jet liked math and science, and all areas of engineering and applied to universities with programs in aeronautics and astronautics. He was accepted to every school he applied to except for one and received a full ride to MIT. It was a day for celebration and he and his mom went out for dinner, a Chinese restaurant with a huge buffet and ate until they couldn't eat anymore. His mom was so proud of him and he was grateful for the recognition, but he knew he couldn't accept the offer. If he had a different life, he would've gone to MIT because it was his first choice. It was his dream. But dreams change as his mom wouldn't do well with him so far away and he couldn't exactly move her to Boston.

In the end, he accepted the offer from University of Montana in Missoula choosing the Applied Science program so he could tailor his studies. But even creating his own major, he wouldn't be studying aeronautics or astronautics. There would be no NASA for him.

SUNDAY NIGHT DINNER was usually a roast, and Emma had outdone herself with a big pot roast—actually three of them—a mountain of mashed potatoes, carrots, gravy, and more, but she turned down Miss Warner's invitation to join them for dinner and disappeared to her rooms.

Briar watched her go, concerned. Emma didn't look well. She just hoped Emma didn't have what Cade and his family had. No one needed a virulent stomach bug.

Miss Warner wanted an early night as well and for the first time since arriving at the ranch, Briar felt restless and bored. She didn't want to be alone with her thoughts, and didn't want to wander the big house, and she most definitely didn't want to go to bed. It was so early, and she was lonely. She hadn't felt truly lonely since arriving, but it hit her hard tonight.

It was a little painful hearing her called Miss Phillips by a cowboy her age. It made her feel old and unattractive. Being pregnant didn't help, either, but no one knew about that. Her jeans were too tight, and she only managed to make them work because she kept the zipper down and didn't tuck in her shirts, letting the tail cover her waist and hips. She felt big and uncomfortable and out of sorts. She wished she had a friend to go to a movie with. Or get an ice cream with. Or go listen to music with. She liked music—country music, R&B, rock and roll. She liked almost everything but being anxious and lonely.

Briar grabbed her coat and headed for the barn. Judas

wasn't the best conversationalist but at least he'd listen, and maybe she could say to him all the fears and needs she was holding in.

❦

JET SAW BRIAR walk past the bunkhouse. With everyone gone, the staff enjoying the last night of their weekend, the bunkhouse was dark, and he was sitting outside on the covered porch, savoring the quiet, always so rare for the bunkhouse.

Briar's boots crunched the gravel as she passed by. She had her head down and hands buried in her coat pocket. He could feel her loneliness tonight and if she was anyone else, he'd call her over, invite her to join him. But she wasn't just anyone. She was Briar Phillips, gorgeous, sexy, bright, fiery. He didn't mind her attitude; he actually rather liked it. He respected a woman who stood her ground and took the world on, brave and bold, practically fearless. But Briar wasn't quite as tough as she projected. He'd begun to see it was almost a façade, a front to keep everyone else from getting close to her. She might act as if she had it all figured out but, when she didn't think anyone was watching, her expression softened and he saw uncertainty in her eyes, a wistfulness that revealed how inexperienced she really was.

A lonely young woman was a problem though on a ranch like this. The last thing wistful, yearning Briar needed was a randy, infatuated cowboy chasing after her. If she didn't know what she was looking for, she'd end up finding trouble, and none of them here at the Sundowner needed trouble.

Once Briar had disappeared into the barn, Jet went inside the bunkhouse and grabbed his laptop to look up some information Miss Warner had requested earlier from him. He was still sitting at the pine dining table when he heard a tentative knock on the door.

Jet stiffened, knowing who it was, knowing it wouldn't be good to have her in here. She was tempting and he was trying hard to play by the rules. She didn't make it easy, though. She didn't even seem to know just how beautiful she was, and how even a man as disciplined as Jet could crave her mouth, those lips so full and lush, he could get lost in them.

She knocked again, a little firmer this time.

Suppressing a sigh, Jet rose and took his time walking to the door. But she was still there when he opened it, standing on the dark porch, her eyes wide, her mouth quivering slightly. "I hope you don't mind me stopping by. Miss Warner went to bed early and I don't know what to do with myself."

He gestured to the table behind him where his laptop sat open. "I'm working. Miss Warner wanted some information so I'm pulling it together."

"Oh." She blinked and silence stretched. Her smile was unsteady. It disappeared and then fluttered back. "Can I just sit in here while you work? I won't bother you. I've got my phone and I'll do some reading of my own. You won't even know I'm here."

That wasn't true, he thought. That would never be true. Jet wouldn't be able to ignore her. It was impossible to ignore her when he felt a painful surge of heat and desire every time he was in the same room with her.

"Please?" she whispered. "I'm having a rough night."

Reluctantly, he opened the door wide and let her in. She glanced around the bunkhouse, clearly curious. The bunkhouse was simply furnished and built for practicality over style. The living room had several long couches and individual chairs. The dining area was the pine table with benches on either side. The kitchen still looked like a relic from the 1930s, the era when the bunkhouse had been built.

"You all sleep in here?" she said, brows pulling together. "It's not that big."

"I have my own room downstairs and there are two bedrooms upstairs, each room has two sets of bunk beds. During summer, the extra staff have their own space with tent cabins and on the other side of the big pasture."

"It takes a lot of people to make this place run," she said.

"It's a big ranch." He folded his arms across his chest, trying to tamp down his impatience. He had work to do and he wasn't in the mood for chitchat, much less chitchat with Briar on an evening when no one else was here and she was looking a little lost and sad. "You should have gone into town with the guys. You could have gotten out for a couple hours."

Her lips quirked. "What you're really saying is that you wish I'd done that instead of come bother you."

"That's not what I mean. We both know Cade doesn't want you hanging out with them, but we also both know he doesn't want you here with me."

"Why?" She held his gaze. "Do you have a reputation for seducing women?"

She was being deliberately provocative and Jet bit down, grinding his back molars to keep from taking the bait. Or from pulling her into his arms and taking her mouth. Her lush, sassy sexy mouth.

"What?" she demanded. "What are you dying to say?"

"I don't want to fight with you," he gritted. "And I don't think it's a good idea for you to stay." He walked back to the door and opened it. "I'm sorry you're lonely and it's rare that I kick a beautiful woman out, but I'm not the one to keep you company."

"We can't be friends?"

"You don't want friends. You want entertainment."

"Wow." Her jaw dropped and she stared at him, green eyes blazing, a mix of anger and hurt. "That wasn't necessary."

No, it wasn't, he thought. She was right about that. But he was doing everything he could to keep her at arm's length when she was begging for attention and comfort. He knew how to provide both, but he also knew it would be temporary, a once off and that would only be even more hurtful later.

"Maybe I'm misreading the situation," he said. "In that case, I apologize. I just know that when a young single woman shows up at a man's place, she's looking for something. Only, Briar, I'm not the one to give it to you. More specifically, I'm not for you."

Her eyes flashed again. "I think you're misunderstanding things here, Jet. I'm not interested in hooking up with you so you can shove your arrogant I'm-too-good-for-you attitude—"

"I've thought a lot of things since you arrived here, but I never once thought that."

"Then why do you look at me that way?"

"What way?"

"Like I'm trouble," she said.

The corner of his mouth tilted. "My apologies. I'm usually better at hiding my feelings."

"So, you do think I'm trouble."

"Briar Phillips, I know you're trouble but that's neither here nor there. I just want to keep my head down, get my work done, and focus on what's important, which is keeping my job."

She gave him a look of hurt and disbelief and then walked past him without saying a word.

Jet closed the door behind her and swore under his breath. That did not go well. He was trying to set boundaries, but instead, Jet knew he'd just made everything worse.

He didn't want to be the bad guy. He didn't like being the bad guy, but having Briar here was not working, not anymore. She was tugging at his heartstrings, appealing to him in a way that made him uncomfortable. The moment Cade returned, Jet would pull him aside and let him know that Briar was an issue—and he hated doing that because Cade would send her away—but what else could he do? Briar was a spark and the longer she remained the more destruction she'd bring. None of them needed trouble, and he didn't want to be here when her spark ignited a fire. He didn't need the fire. He didn't need to burn.

He'd burned before and paid the price. He was here trying to salvage his reputation and redeem his name. Once he'd had a career and a bright future, but he'd lost it all. Feeling too much, feeling responsible, feeling guilty had made him cross the line. The police hadn't made any arrests. The man who'd killed his mother had never served any time. Everyone knew who'd done it, but the lack of forensic evidence meant Larry Mason went free. So, Jet had taken justice into his own hands. He didn't beat Larry to death—he was stopped before he could do that—but he made Larry hurt. He made Larry suffer, and Jet, who then lost everything, had no regrets. Confronted with the same choice, he'd do it again.

Chapter Four

Briar slept poorly, angry with herself for stopping by the bunkhouse, and angry with Jet for making her feel terrible about herself. She wasn't a femme fatale or a black widow spider. She didn't poison or devour men. She actually had very little experience with them.

It took forever to fall asleep, but Briar woke early, just as she always did. Briar wished she could sleep in for once, but it just didn't happen. She headed downstairs and made herself some tea and was still in the kitchen at the counter drinking her tea when Emma entered the kitchen. Briar could see immediately that Emma was ill, and Briar, who didn't have a lot of skill as a cook, had nursed her dad through a few illnesses, knew how to manage things, having taken over the household chores after her mom died.

"You have to go back to bed," Briar said firmly. "Not just for your own good, but to protect Miss Warner."

Emma, who didn't often relinquish her role in the house, nodded miserably. "You're right. But I hate abandoning my responsibilities—"

"You're not. I'm forcing you to bed." Briar smiled kindly. "You have no choice. Now go rest, I've got this."

Emma was too weak to protest and returned to the ground floor apartment she shared with Willis in a wing off the kitchen and Briar put on an apron and got to work.

By the time Miss Warner came down for breakfast, Briar had already beaten the eggs and popped a slice of wheat toast in the toaster. Briar emerged from the kitchen to tell Miss Warner she'd sent Emma back to bed since she wasn't well, and that Briar would take over housekeeping and cooking until Emma was better.

"It's a lot for one person to do," Miss Warner said as she slowly and carefully sat down at the head of the dining room table.

Briar moved to help her with her chair, but Miss Warner waved her away and Briar went to the kitchen to get the pot of coffee. "Emma does it on her own," she said, returning and filling Miss Warner's delicate china cup.

"Yes, but she's had years to learn how. You've just arrived."

"I've been here over a week," Briar answered, "and I might not be an experienced cook, but I know Emma's routine, and I helped at home. After my mom died, I took over a lot of things—cleaning, and organizing things, even paying some of the bills, since my dad wasn't good at getting them out on time. I can make a few basic things, too, eggs, grilled cheese, tuna sandwiches. Tacos and Sloppy Joes."

"Glad we won't starve then," Miss Warner said, fighting

a smile.

"Let me go get those eggs going."

The eggs came out fine and the toast wasn't burned, and Miss Warner ate her eggs, toast, and half grapefruit without complaint. When Briar returned to touch up Miss Warner's coffee, Miss Warner gestured to an empty chair at the table. "Why don't you sit and tell me a little about your parents," Miss Warner said. "I know very little about you. You haven't shared much."

"There's not a lot to say. My dad's a pastor, and my mom was a homemaker when I was little, but after I started school, she returned to work. She was killed in a car accident when I was fifteen."

"I would think that's a hard age to lose a parent."

"I think it would be hard to lose a parent at any age." Briar hesitated before adding, "But I do have regrets about how I acted then, and what I put her through. I was mad at Mom when she left for work that day. I was mad she was always working, mad because I was fifteen and pissed off at the world. I said mean things as she left. I've spent years wishing I could take it all back. I wish I'd said I loved her instead."

"Was the weather bad?"

"No. A car ran a red light in downtown Marietta. Broadsided her just two blocks from her office."

"That's terrible."

"I've had a hard time moving forward. I can't forgive

myself."

"Your anger didn't kill her," said Jet, entering the room and removing his cowboy hat.

Briar tensed and she refused to look at him even as he walked to the table and placed a stack of mail in front of Miss Warner.

Her stomach knotted, resentment burning in her. He was the last person she wanted to see today. "You don't know that," Briar flashed, embarrassed that Jet had overheard the conversation, and even more annoyed that he'd inject himself into it. After last night, she wanted nothing to do with him. After last night she'd lost all respect for him.

But Miss Warner had no idea they'd had words last night and welcomed Jet. "Get some coffee," she told Jet. "And join us. I know you lost your mom, too. I'm sure you relate."

She turned to Briar, adding, "Being angry is part of being a teenager. I've had plenty of teenagers on this ranch—probably none more angry that your brother—and that's just part of growing up. Puberty isn't pleasant. I'm glad I only went through it once."

Briar struggled to smile even as she rose. "If you'll excuse me. I should get busy."

Miss Warner put her hand on Briar's to stop her. "Stay. There's no rush."

Briar swallowed her frustration and slowly sat back down as Jet returned with his coffee. If Miss Warner wasn't sitting there, Briar might have thrown something at Jet. Her water.

The pitcher of orange juice. A heavy crystal vase. But Miss Warner was here, and Briar respected her too much to create a scene.

Jet sat down, taking the place directly across the table from Briar. He looked comfortable and calm, completely at ease. "When your mom walked out the door that day, she knew you loved her—"

"It's really none of your business," Briar said under her breath.

Jet had the audacity to smile at her. "Your mom knew you. She loved you and understood you were a teenager full of hormones and emotions. Just as she didn't doubt your dad's love, she didn't ever doubt yours."

"Yes," Miss Warner said nodding. "This is an important lesson. One can't live in a state of guilt. Guilt is a terrible thing. It's like acid. It erodes the soul." Miss Warner took Briar's hand and held it firmly. "Focus on the love, not the pain. We can't help but have pain. We're human. But you can't let the pain win. You fight pain by leaning into the love."

Pain splintered in Briar's chest, and she felt her eyes burn. She squeezed Miss Warner's hand back. "Thank you. I like that."

"Well, I like you," Miss Warner said, a husky note entering her voice. "I don't know how it's happened, but you and Cade are two of my favorite people."

If Briar was a more demonstrative person, she might have

thrown herself into Miss Warner. But Briar wasn't, and to be fair, neither was Miss Warner. So, Briar managed a watery smile and felt a rush of gratitude.

Miss Warner's small phone rang then, and she looked down at the number. "It's Cade," she announced. "I'm going to take it."

It took her a moment to answer the call as her hand shook, but then she pressed the right button and found the speaker button and had him on the line. "Cade, how are you? How is everyone?"

"Grace is better now and I'm starting to feel better. I'm worried about Bee. She said she's fine but she's looking rather pale."

"That's not good."

"She has so much energy and never slows down, but she's dragging now."

"I hate to hear that. Stay put until everyone's better," Miss Warner said. "And take care of your MerriBee. Make sure she gets TLC."

"You know I will."

"It's a nasty bug, and there's no point passing this around, and so, while you're missed, you're not missed that much."

Cade snorted and Briar smiled, amused. Dorothy Warner was pretty amazing. Glancing up, her gaze accidentally met Jet's and then held, her smile fading.

She and Jet were not friends, but she hadn't expected his

roughness last night. She hadn't expected such harsh words or a rude dismissal. It had been incredibly hurtful, and she'd fought tears as she'd gone to bed, and even this morning she felt ... betrayed. Why she felt betrayed was beyond her as they weren't close, but somehow she hadn't expected it of him.

Briar used the opportunity to quickly collect the breakfast dishes and return to the kitchen, leaving Jet with Miss Warner. But as she began to wash the dishes she heard footsteps, the heavy kind, the kind in cowboy boots, and she straightened.

"I will not be rude to you in front of Miss Warner," she said tightly, "but we're not friends and I have nothing to say to you. Please just stay out of my way and I'll stay out of yours."

"I don't blame you for being upset," he said from behind her, placing his empty cup on the counter just to the left of the sink. "I was rude. I apologize."

"Apology not accepted. Please go."

He should have disappeared then, taken his hat and run away, but instead he stayed put and laughed, a low husky rumble that made her insides feel funny and her chest tighten and ache.

She spun to face him, the soapy sponge clenched in her hand. "I'm not messing around. You better leave before I kick your—" She broke off, cheeks flushing as Miss Warner walked in.

Miss Warner looked form one to the other. "Whatever has happened set your differences aside as I need you two to work together. With Emma sick, and Briar taking on more responsibility, I'll require Jet helping here as much as he can." She looked at Jet, a silver eyebrow lifting. "Can you manage your work and helping here, too? Briar could manage if it was just me, but I won't have her cooking for all the boys."

"I agree," Jet said. "I'll happily share kitchen duty," he added giving Briar a smug smile.

"I don't need his help," Briar said, focusing on Miss Warner and only Miss Warner. "I know how to make easy things and it won't be as good as Emma's cooking, but no one will starve."

"But I have no problem pitching in," Jet said. "Once I finish up my work, I'll come back this afternoon and will make dinner for everyone—"

"No," Briar snapped, slapping the wet sponge on the counter. "Tonight is taco night—"

"Tuesday is usually taco night," Jet interrupted helpfully.

She glared at him and then turned to Miss Warner. "I can handle feeding nine men. For Pete's sake, tacos are foolproof. Ground beef, taco seasoning, hard shells, and lettuce, tomatoes and cheese. I used to help with lunch after cowboy church and everyone liked my tacos. So, there's no need to drag Jet up this evening. He has important things to do elsewhere, and honestly, as much as he wants to contribute, he'd just be in the way." She glanced at Jet then and gave him a sickly sweet smile.

He smiled back, a glint in his blue eyes, his face still annoyingly gorgeous. It would be so much easier to hate him if he wasn't handsome and interesting and if her pulse didn't jump when she heard his voice or saw him, even at a distance.

"Not sure what's happened, but I'm the boss here and I'm making the decisions," Miss Warner said. "Briar cooks tonight. Jet cooks tomorrow. Now both of you, sort this out before you give me a headache."

IN THE EARLY afternoon, following Miss Warner's lunch, Briar made a cup of tea and added one of Emma's little snickerdoodle cookies to the plate and carried both to Emma in her apartment, even though Emma had a small kitchen of her own.

Knocking on the door, Briar opened it a crack and called in to Emma. "It's me, Briar. I brought you some tea and a cookie. Can I come in?"

"Yes, dear. Just don't get close. I don't want to get you sick."

Briar walked through the empty living room, past the kitchen and dining nook to the bedroom at the back. She peeked around the bedroom door and there was Emma in bed, quite pale with watery pink eyes and a very red nose.

"Poor Emma!" she said, approaching the bed with the cup and saucer. "Have you had anything to eat today? Can I get you some soup or toast?"

"Jet brought me peanut butter toast earlier," Emma said, sounding embarrassed. "And now you're here with tea. I am being spoiled."

Jet had already been here? With peanut butter toast? Briar was beginning to think he might be nicer than he let on.

"You should be spoiled," Briar said. "You work so hard here." Briar placed the tea on the nightstand, close to Emma's elbow. "How do you feel?"

"Achy. My throat hurts. But I'm sure I'll be better tomorrow."

"I don't think you will be," Briar answered. "Colds take three or four days usually, don't they? And even little colds can get worse if you don't take care of yourself. I think you should stay in bed the next few days—"

"I can't do that," Emma protested, lifting a tissue to her nose and gently blowing it. "We're low on groceries and I need to do my shopping—"

"I can do all of that."

"But you don't know where I shop or what I need."

"I'll figure it out, and I'm sure someone will help me." Briar gently patted Emma's shoulder. "Now how about some soup? I know you have a freezer stocked with all your homemade recipes. What sounds best? I'll heat it up and bring it to you now—"

"Not hungry now," Emma said. "But thank you."

"What about for dinner?"

"You don't have to do that. Focus on Miss Warner. I have some soup here I can heat up for myself. Now go, my dear, before I give you my germs."

❦

MONDAY NIGHT TACOS was a success, at least from a feeding hungry people standpoint. But she went to bed exhausted and woke up still tired. She worried for a moment she, too, was coming down sick, but she didn't have a sore throat and she wasn't achy. She'd just worked all day yesterday, and after making three meals for Miss Warner, dust mopping the hardwood floors, washing the lower living room windows, which had been splattered by rain, and then cooking tacos for all the guys—how on earth did nine men go through four pounds of ground beef and three dozen taco shells?—she'd been left with a very dirty kitchen, with skillets covering the stove. Emma never needed that many dishes. Emma was a pro.

If Briar wasn't so stubborn, she might have accepted Jet's offer to do the dishes last night but she saw his expression when he entered the kitchen, a combination of shock and awe, especially as he took in the skillet-covered stove and she sent him away. But then, Briar had a history of cutting off her nose to spite her own face.

Someday she'd learn, but clearly, the someday hadn't

arrived yet.

Downstairs, Briar started the coffee and then set the breakfast table, but when Miss Warner called the kitchen's intercom, she told Briar she'd like her to join her for breakfast and so Briar made them both eggs and toast and poured each of them a glass of milk as well.

Miss Warner frowned at her milk glass, but Briar wasn't having any of it. "It's good for your bones," Briar said, sitting down.

"You're getting awfully bossy," Miss Warner replied severely, but she had a little twinkle in her eye and Briar just smiled at her.

"I have to take care of you. You're the queen of Sundowner Ranch, and I won't let anything happen on my watch."

Miss Warner carefully scooped up eggs with her spoon, an easier endeavor than using her fork these days. "Nothing will happen to me. I have at least ten years in me yet."

Briar smiled at her. "That's good. I'm getting rather fond of you and I'm awful at goodbyes."

Miss Warner studied her a moment. "Cade implied you had a history of being difficult. I've never once seen that side of you."

Briar tore her toast wedge in half and took a bite and then swallowed. "That's because I'm nice around you."

Miss Warner laughed. "You're very smart, that's the problem. Smart women need to be challenged. Did you go to college, Briar?"

"I did not. By the time I graduated I didn't have the grades for it."

"In *any* subject?"

Briar hesitated, picturing high school, picturing her not going to class, picturing sitting out on the picnic table—even in winter—smoking cigarettes, acting bored and oh, so cool. "I didn't try," she said. "I rarely went to class."

"So how did you graduate?"

"I'd look at the book the night before a big test and then I'd show up and get just enough right to pass."

"You were playing a game."

Briar's gaze met Miss Warner's. Miss Warner's expression was knowing. Shrewd.

"I suppose I was," Briar admitted. "I would do as little as possible but make sure I didn't fail. I just wanted to be done with school and I knew my dad wouldn't allow me to be a dropout. So, I got my diploma—"

"Barely."

"Barely," Briar agreed. "But my report card was littered with Cs and Ds. No university would take me." *I made sure of that.*

"It's been how many years since then?" Miss Warner had finished her eggs and she slowly spread Emma's homemade jam on her slice of toast.

Briar watched Miss Warner's hand quivering as she applied the jam. She suddenly felt close to tears. Miss Warner was not young. Miss Warner would not live forever. But Miss Warner should. She was really remarkable. "Four," Briar said, blinking hard.

"Any regrets?"

Briar managed a smile. Smiles always held tears back. "Thousands." She quickly dabbed beneath her eyes with her linen napkin. "Did you go to college?"

"No, I didn't. But I like to read. I like following the news and current events. I subscribe to a lot of magazines, *National Geographic*, *Smithsonian*, *New Yorker* and I find it's good to keep learning. Keep the body active, keep the mind active, don't become complacent."

"What do you do for exercise?"

"Well, as you've seen, I'm not as active as I used to be, which is a shame, because until a couple years ago, I was walking a lot every day, I was riding—"

"As in horseback riding?"

"Absolutely. I was in a saddle before I could walk. I love to ride."

"I do, too. That's my first love. It's what I want to do. Work with horses, train, maybe breed them. If I ever have the opportunity, that's what I'll do."

"Why wouldn't you have the opportunity? You have the goals. Now make it happen."

"If only it was that easy," Briar said quietly.

"Nothing is easy—not true—doing nothing is easy. Doing something, now, that takes guts."

Briar did laundry and changed the sheets on the beds and was thinking about what she'd make for lunch and dinner, when Jet entered the kitchen with a pile of magazines and envelopes. He nodded at her, and she nodded at him, and he passed through the kitchen to the dining room and beyond.

She wasn't collected on the inside. She felt hot and cold, prickly really. It was hard to stay mad at him, hard to not speak to him. She hadn't realized how much she'd enjoyed his company until there wasn't any company or conversation.

Perhaps they could have been friends if she felt platonic feelings for him. But there was nothing platonic in her racing pulse or the disconcerting fizzy painful feeling she got when he was near.

Feeling like an emotional basket case Briar took herself to her room, had a lovely bath, and then lay down for a nap. She hadn't expected to sleep, but after tossing around feeling fretful and frustrated, she closed her eyes and when she woke, it was almost five.

Briar quickly dressed and pulled her long hair into a ponytail and hurried to the kitchen to start dinner, but Jet was there with everything in control. He had a tray of steaks seasoned generously with salt and pepper. While they sat, coming to room temperature he washed and prepped twelve huge russet potatoes before putting them in the hot oven.

Briar was more than a little impressed by his efficiency in

the kitchen. He managed dinner the same way he saddled his horse—there were very few wasted movements. "I'm sorry I'm late," she said. "I fell asleep—"

He turned, surprised to see her. "Tonight's my night to cook. You didn't need to worry."

"I wasn't sure if you'd remember," she said, feeling foolish.

"I never forget." His brilliant blue gaze locked with hers.

She wasn't sure what that meant, but heat washed through her, and her cheeks were already hot, burned. Her lips, suddenly sensitive, tingled. Shivers danced up her spine. She didn't hate him. But she wasn't herself around him. She didn't know what she was anymore.

Jet stepped past her, walked through to the mudroom and then outside. She followed him to the mudroom door and watched as he fired up the huge barbecue. She was still standing there as he returned to the kitchen.

"I've got this," he said, forced to stop in the mudroom corridor since there was no way past her without physically moving her.

She stepped aside and let him walk past. "What else will we be having?" Briar asked as he returned to the sink and rinsed lettuce.

"Salad and garlic bread."

"Need help?"

"No. I'm in good shape here. There's no point us tripping over each other. Why don't you go see Judas or call your friends or relax? I'm sure there's something you could do that would be more fun."

Briar hesitated, that pinch of pain in her chest again. She didn't blame him for dismissing her. She'd done the same thing to him the day before.

But seeing as there were no friends to call, Briar went to the barn, but Judas wasn't there. She almost panicked and then saw him from the corner of her eye, standing at the paddock fence watching her.

He shook his head at her, and she smiled and went to him. "Someone let you out to play," she said, facing his shoulder and petting his neck, and then giving a scratch just behind his hear. "You liked it, too. You're smiling."

Judas wasn't the only horse in the grassy enclosure. She saw Jet's horse and a half dozen others. Jet probably freed Judas, making more points with her gelding, but she was pleased he'd done that. She'd been so busy lately she wasn't spending enough time with her horse, and he was used to attention, a lot of attention.

As she returned to the house to shower and change for dinner, she got a ping notifying her of a new text. She checked the text as she reached the house. It was from the adoption agency in Bozeman. They were checking in on her. *Hope your pregnancy is going well. We're thinking of you and are here for you. We know you want what's best for your beautiful baby.*

Her legs went weak, her stomach somersaulted, and Briar climbed the stairs to her second-floor bedroom slowly. Part of her wished she'd never given them her contact information, but another part appreciated the check-in, and the reminder she still needed to make a decision.

Time was beginning to run out.

In her room, she pulled the pamphlets and adoption paperwork out of her nightstand's top drawer. She'd gotten them from a different agency in Bozeman, this one specialized in open adoptions. Like her birth mother, Briar could select the couple for her baby. She could meet them and even decide how much contact she'd want with the family after she handed the baby over. They'd be at the hospital when she gave birth and could even be the first to hold her baby.

Briar put the paperwork back in the drawer.

She wanted to be the first to hold her baby. How did someone do this? How did you carry a baby and then give it up?

Nauseous and heartsick, Briar stripped and took a shower, washed her long hair and had just enough time to put it in a wet braid before dressing and heading down to dinner.

But downstairs, Briar's thoughts were far from calm. With it just her and Miss Warner, Briar found it hard to eat, never mind make conversation.

If she was going to give the baby up for adoption, she needed to start looking for the right family. She didn't want to rush the process. That would only make her feel more anxious, and guilty, and that was the last thing she needed.

If she was going to keep the baby, she needed a plan.

What would she do? Where would she live? And glancing in Miss Warner's direction, Briar knew she couldn't live here. She couldn't—wouldn't—live off Miss Warner's generosity. It was a sure way to alienate her brother and lose her own self-respect.

After dinner, Briar put their dishes in the sink to soak and then joined Miss Warner in the family room. At the end of *Wheel of Fortune*, Briar dished Miss Warner one of the brownies Jet had made—apparently Jet could do everything—and topped it with a scoop of vanilla ice cream. Returning to the family room, Miss Warner frowned when she saw that Briar wasn't having any dessert.

"What's wrong?" Miss Warner asked as Briar sat down. "Jet's brownies are delicious."

"I'm sure they are, but I haven't had much of an appetite tonight."

"Coming down sick?"

"No, I don't think."

"Are we working you too hard?"

"No. I just have a lot on my mind and I'm trying to figure out the future. It's not easy after spending the last four years pretending there wouldn't be one."

"I like that you're taking your future seriously. You're too bright to spend your twenties doing nothing." Miss Warner muted the television. "What about Jet? Are you and he still having a tiff?"

Briar pursed her lips, remembering how her mother

would use that word. "It's better," she said. "He took Judas outside today. Let him run around."

"Good. No horse wants to be cooped up all the time."

"I know. I meant to ask where I could take him. It slipped my mind."

"What's more important than your horse?" Miss Warner asked, sounding appalled.

Briar shook her head. "Nothing, I guess."

"What else?" Miss Warner prompted, setting her dessert bowl aside. "I've been watching you these past few days and you have every right to feel how you want to feel, but I don't think you're a naturally moody girl, but you're troubled about something. You look as if you have the weight of the world on your shoulders, and I might be ninety and clueless when it comes to technology, but I can be a good listener."

Briar reached over and covered Miss Warner's hand. "Thank you. That means a lot to me."

She removed her hand and Miss Warner lifted one imperious eyebrow. "Is that it? That is all you can say?"

Briar's lips twitched. Initially she'd resented being forced to stay at the main house, but she'd come to admire Miss Warner immensely and looked forward to seeing her every day. Miss Warner was perceptive and didn't mince words. She said what she thought, meant what she said, and for Briar, it was a relief. She preferred people to be direct, and appreciated plain speaking, although to be fair, Cade spoke a little too plainly at times.

"I have to make a big decision," Briar said, gathering her thoughts. "I came here because I needed Cade's input, but now I'm not sure I want his opinion. I've realized I don't actually want anyone's opinions because ultimately the decision is mine and I'm the one to have to live with it."

"That makes perfect sense," Miss Warner said. "So, what do you want now? What do you need?"

That was a good question and Briar hadn't gotten that far. She thought about it until she had an answer. "Support," she said simply. "I hope whatever I decide, I'll be supported in my decision."

"Why wouldn't you be?"

"Not everyone might agree with what I choose."

"It is *your* life, Briar, and as you said earlier, you're the one that has to live with the decision … unless it affects someone else?"

"Not directly, no."

"If it truly is a hard decision, it's going to be painful no matter what you choose, so choose the decision you can live with, not just the day you make it, but every day after. Life can be long. Regret can be endless."

Briar looked at Miss Warner, really looked at her, and it crossed her mind that perhaps Miss Warner had regrets of her own. Perhaps there had been different choices she could have made, or would have made. Perhaps there might have been love, and a family.

Instead, she remained single and held her own in what

was very much a man's world. But she'd done it, protecting the ranch and earning the admiration of her staff as well as the neighboring ranchers.

Briar had grown up not knowing who she was supposed to be. But for the first time in her life, she knew the type of woman she wanted to be.

Brave like Miss Warner. Direct, strong, but also compassionate. A woman who wasn't afraid to take risks. A woman who lived by her own rules.

Briar leaned forward and kissed Miss Warner's cheek. "Thank you," she said, emotion deepening her voice.

Miss Warner caught her hand. "For what?"

"For being you."

Chapter Five

WEDNESDAY MORNING BRIAR woke up slowly and stretched before checking the time. Five fifteen. She'd slept in for a whole fifteen minutes today. The thought made her smile. She snuggled under her covers and dozed until she couldn't put off using the bathroom any longer, but when she did, she noticed blood. Not a terrible amount, but still, it scared her.

Back in bed, she tried to stay calm as she did a symptom search on her phone but every article she read indicated spotting in the third trimester could be problematic and recommended she see a doctor as soon as possible. She didn't even have a doctor nearby and hadn't even seen one regularly in Marietta. Briar didn't know if she should try to go to a local hospital or call around. If MerriBee was here, Briar would ask her, but Briar was hesitant to disturb MerriBee because it'd mean disclosing the pregnancy and no one knew.

But there might not be a pregnancy if Briar didn't take action.

Briar waited until six to text her sister-in-law. She

watched the time obsessively. The moment it was six she texted MerriBee, *Can you call me please, if possible?*

Her phone rang moments later. "Are you okay?" MerriBee asked.

"I think so. Actually, I don't know." Briar took a deep breath. "MerriBee, do nurses take a Hippocratic oath? To do no wrong and keep patients' information private?"

"We have the Nightingale pledge," MerriBee answered. "But I'm very good at keeping confidential information confidential."

"Even from my brother?"

"Are you in danger, Briar?" MerriBee asked gently.

"I'm not, but someone else might be."

"I see."

But Briar knew MerriBee didn't understand, or couldn't, not without more information. "I'm pregnant," Briar said in a rush. "Close to twenty-eight weeks. I came here to figure out what I was going to do, discuss my options with Cade, but he's been away, and everything has been fine until today. When I woke up this morning, I discovered I'm bleeding. I've been online reading and everything I read recommended I get in to see a doctor immediately."

"I agree, yes."

"But I don't know where to go. I didn't know if you had any suggestions. I could go to the hospital in Sheridan—if that's the closest to me—or…"

"Sheridan has the nearest, most comprehensive medical

facility. Are you cramping? Does your back ache? How do you feel right now?"

"If it wasn't for the blood, I wouldn't know anything was wrong."

"That's good. Is there a lot?"

"No."

MerriBee was silent a moment, thinking. "I tell you what, get ready to head to Sheridan and I'm going to make some calls. If I can't get you in to any of the doctors I know, then go to ER at Sheridan Memorial on Fifth Street."

"Emma is sick, so I'll make Miss Warner's breakfast and then take off."

"Miss Warner is fine making her own breakfast. I want you to get ready to go, okay? I'll call or text you an address as soon as I know where I'm sending you."

"Okay. I'll be on the road soon then."

"One more thing," MerriBee said gently. "I'm not sure you should be driving. Is there no one that could give you a ride?"

Briar thought about her possibilities, which was mainly Jet, and ruled them out. "No, I don't think so."

※

BUT JET WAS there in the kitchen when Briar came downstairs. He'd started the coffee for Miss Warner, and he was waiting for Briar, his heavy sheepskin coat on. "MerriBee reached out to me," he said. "I'm going to drive you to

Sheridan."

Briar flushed. "That's not necessary."

"If you're not feeling well, the last thing you need to do is navigate strange roads." He gave her a look as if he expected an argument. "Besides, I have some errands to run in Sheridan, and I've already talked to Miss Warner. She knows we'll both be gone this morning so there's nothing to worry about."

For once, Briar was too anxious to argue with him. "I don't know how long my appointment will be."

"That's fine. The ranch is full of people who can help, whether in the kitchen or elsewhere. You don't need to worry about anything right now but getting to my truck."

Briar was too relieved to have a ride to say anything but thank you. She followed him out to his black truck, which he'd parked in front of the house. He reached past her to open the passenger door for her.

"Thank you," she said, stepping up and in.

"You're welcome."

Briar buckled up and watched as he shrugged his heavy lambskin jacket off and placed it on the backseat before starting the engine. He looked big, powerful, and commanding, as if he'd taken charge many times in his life.

"Do you have an address for me?" he asked, reversing and then pulling onto the gravel drive.

"MerriBee is making some calls right now. She said to head to the hospital for now, and if she can get me into someone else, she'll call me with that address."

He glanced at her as they left the ranch outbuildings behind. "You okay?"

She nodded but couldn't smile. She felt numb and truly scared. If something was wrong, she wasn't sure she could handle it. The baby had to be fine. She was so far along now she couldn't imagine any other outcome than a healthy baby.

"I'm glad you reached out to MerriBee," Jet said, ten minutes later as they approached the highway. "She knows all the best doctors. You'll be in good hands."

Briar nodded and looked out of the window, trying not to think, trying not to worry, trying to stay relaxed in case that would help.

Jet put on the radio, choosing a channel she wouldn't have normally listened to, but the classical music was soothing, and he kept the volume low. Briar wouldn't have figured Jet to be a guy who liked symphonies but obviously she didn't know that much about him. She glanced at him, wondering who he was, not Jet Manning Sundowner Ranch hand, but Jet the person.

They reached the outskirts of Sheridan and Briar gave him the address that had come in from MerriBee, and they were soon taking an exit into downtown. Within minutes they were there, and Briar wasn't sure what kind of building it would be, or what kind of signage would be out front. Fortunately, it was just a nondescript medical building, a box of a building, two stories tall with dark tinted windows.

Jet pulled in front, and she climbed out. "You have my number, call me when you need me."

"I will. Thank you."

"Feel free to call if you just need someone to wait with you."

She looked into his face and saw the concern in his eyes, and it meant a lot to her. "Thank you, I will."

Inside the medical suite, there was paperwork to fill out, a lot of paperwork, and insurance information Briar couldn't give as she didn't have insurance. But the receptionist told her not to worry, that it was understood that it was a cash visit, covered by MerriBee, and Briar's eyes stung, overcome by emotion. Things were tough financially. Doctor's appointments were expensive. It was the main reason she hadn't seen a doctor more often, concerned about the cost, but today she didn't need to worry about that. She just needed to know if the baby was okay.

It was an hour wait to be taken to an exam room, and then another twenty minutes in the exam room before the doctor appeared. But once Dr. Drew entered the room, he immediately put Briar to ease and wasted no time checking the baby's heartbeat and then performing a low-resolution ultrasound which wasn't harmful for the baby.

Briar watched the computer screen intently as the doctor performed the ultrasound, sliding the transducer over her gel-covered abdomen. She'd had an ultrasound early in the first trimester and it had been interesting but this ... this was so different. This was a baby. Head, shoulders, chest, hips, legs. And how those little legs kicked. A hand moved, tiny fingers flexing. Enthralled, she couldn't look away from the screen. She'd known she was pregnant but this ... this was a revelation. This was her person. Her own human.

"Everything looks wonderful," Dr. Drew said, holding the transducer still so they could watch the lovely movements. "She looks perfect." The doctor removed the transducer, wiped the gel off, and put it away.

Briar sat partway up. "She's a girl?"

"You didn't know?"

Briar shook her head. "No. I haven't had a lot of appointments." She touched the tip of her tongue to her upper lip, stunned, and trying to process it all. "You're sure?"

"She gave us a full frontal," he said.

Wow.

A girl.

A daughter.

"You're getting to the point you need to stay on top of your care. I'd like to see you again in two weeks, just to be sure, and from then, once a month until we hit June, and then it'll be every week until she arrives." The doctor wiped the gel off Briar's stomach and helped her sit up. "Make sure you're eating the right foods, drinking plenty of liquid. Avoid caffeine—"

"I am, can't even stand the smell of coffee anymore."

Dr. Drew smiled sympathetically. "Was it a rough first

trimester?"

She pulled her blouse over her middle and tugged up her waistband which she no longer zipped all the way closed. "I was sick all the time."

"That might be why you haven't put on a lot of weight. But from now on, your baby should be putting on a pound a month. We want to see her grow. You need to take care of yourself, which means you're taking care of her."

Briar nodded, still trying to process it all. "I will and thank you so much. I can't tell you how much better I feel. When I saw the blood—"

"Your reaction was perfectly normal, and you were smart to come in. Spotting usually happens more often in the first trimester than the third, but it's not unheard of. I'm glad MerriBee sent you in." He scribbled notes on the chart and, pausing, glanced at Briar. "How do you know her?"

"She's my sister-in-law. My brother's wife."

"Well, she's a treasure. We're lucky to have her here in Sheridan. Please be sure to give her my best."

"I will and thank you so much for working me into your schedule. I know you did that as a favor for MerriBee, but I'm really grateful."

"Happy to do so. Now, I want you to schedule an appointment for two weeks from now, and then mid-April, mid-May, and weekly from the start of June. Also, pick up prenatal vitamins at the pharmacy. Keep my number handy in case anything happens. There's no reason for you to worry, and if something is concerning, just pop in, and we'll have a look and can stay on top of things."

Briar nodded again and, after thanking him once more, he left the room. As she put her socks and boots back on, she found herself smiling. She'd arrived feeling so scared, and now she was ... a mom to a girl.

Her pregnancy was fine and her baby, her little girl, was perfect. Elated, Briar sent MerriBee a text. *Everything is okay. Dr. Drew said she looks perfect. Thank you soooo much for your help today. Can't wait to see you soon and give you the biggest hug!*

JET PULLED UP to the small medical complex in Sheridan and there was Briar, on the curb already waiting for him. She wasn't smiling but she no longer had that pinched look on her face.

He parked and came around to open her door for her. "Everything okay?" he asked.

"Yes."

Her relief was palpable and that reassured him. He wasn't sure what was wrong, and he refused to speculate. "Are you hungry?" he asked, climbing behind the wheel.

She started to shake her head and then nodded. "Yes."

He pushed a paper bag toward her. "Not sure if you like them, but I picked up some breakfast burritos on the way. I also have some orange juice. Help yourself."

She did, too, and it was gratifying to see her relax and

eat. He didn't try to make conversation, either. He'd worried about her all morning, and he didn't know why he cared so much. He'd told himself it was because she was young and Cade's sister, but in his heart, he wasn't so sure that was the correct answer. At the same time, he wasn't interested in exploring his feelings. Emotions were not his strength. In fact, previous girlfriends would say he had no feelings but that wasn't true. He could feel, he just didn't like to. Emotions complicated everything. It was better to make decisions rationally, to use one's head, not one's heart.

It was why he was still single. Jet had no intention of ever marrying, either. He only saw marriage as a necessity if someone wanted children and he didn't. He didn't get lonely, and didn't crave company, male or female. Living in the bunkhouse squashed the need for socializing. When he wanted something physically, he worked out or met up with someone in Sheridan who liked seeing him but had reasons for not wanting to be in a relationship. It was really an ideal situation, and he appreciated his freedom.

"Where are you from?" she asked. "Were you raised around here?"

"No. Montana."

"That's where I'm from."

He couldn't help smiling. "I know. You're Pastor Phillips's kid, remember?"

She grimaced. "I'm not a kid."

He checked his smile. "Just teasing you."

"In that case, where did you grow up? It's a big state."

"I was born in Great Falls and raised in Butte. I finished high school in Polson and went to college in Missoula." His gaze met hers briefly. "Is that enough detail for you?"

She laughed, a gurgle of pleasure that caught him off guard. He felt a stab of sensation, a tightening in his chest that was as unfamiliar as it was unwelcome.

"You are a true Montanan." Briar grinned at him. "Probably raised on venison and huckleberries."

Such a smart-ass, he thought, the warmth in his chest spreading through him. She was far too tempting, her mouth far too soft and full. It would be easy to get lost in her, easy to forget why she was off-limits, but Jet had only lost control once and it had life-changing consequences and that wouldn't happen again. He wouldn't let down his guard, not even when she smiled like that, with so much light in her eyes that she shone from the inside out. "Close. Raised on Hamburger Helper and orange Jell-O, but I do like a good steak."

"I can tell. You grilled a good steak last night."

"Not sure I believe you. Miss Warner said you didn't eat anything."

Briar's eyes narrowed. "Is she reporting on me?"

"No, but she cares about you. Quite a bit. When I told her I'd brought you into Sheridan, she asked me to update her as soon as possible." He glanced at her before returning his focus to the road. "Sounds like you two had a serious conversation last night and she's wanting to be supportive."

Suddenly Briar's eyes filled with tears, and she put a fist to her mouth and held it there. One tear fell and then another.

He glanced at her again. "Did I say the wrong thing?"

She shook her head. "No. It's just that ... she listened. She heard me."

He wanted so badly to take her hand, or comfort her, but she wasn't his to comfort. He swallowed the first words that came to mind, and then the next. Finally, he said, "I know we didn't exactly hit it off that first day, but if you need anything, I am here."

WHEN THEY RETURNED to the ranch, Briar discovered she'd been excused from kitchen duty and two cowboys named Ace and Guy were in the kitchen coming up with a plan for dinner.

Ace gave Briar a very warm smile while Guy just shyly tipped his head. Briar immediately preferred Guy to cocky Ace who reminded her far too much of Garrett.

Briar put on the teakettle and made two cups of tea, one for Emma and one for herself. She tiptoed into Emma's apartment not wanting to wake her if she was asleep. But Emma was sitting up in bed, watching TV.

"How are you feeling?" Briar asked, giving Emma a cup of tea.

"Better. I'm bored, though. I guess that's a good sign. But what about you? Miss Warner said you had to go to the hospital today."

Briar sat down in the chair by the television. "No, not the hospital. I did go see a doctor but everything's great. I'm great." She took a quick sip of her tea. "When does Willis come home? He's been gone a long time."

"This weekend. And I agree. I was excited for him to go see his family, but I'm ready for him to come home."

Fifteen minutes later when Briar went to her room, she grabbed the adoption paperwork and a pen and carried it to the chair by the window and taking a deep breath she began to fill it out, blinking hard to keep tears from falling.

This was being responsible, she told herself, getting up once to blow her nose before returning to the chair to finish the forms.

She was determined to make good choices from now on.

Be selfless. And strong.

She would make sure her daughter had the best life possible.

She would.

And yet ... oh, how hard this was being strong. How hard it was to do the right thing.

She was still wiping away tears when a knock sounded on her door. Briar rubbed the tissue beneath her eyes and went to the door.

It was Jet.

She sniffled and tried to smile. "Hey."

He entered the room, brow furrowed, creases at his eyes. "Do you need to go to the doctor?"

Briar shook her head and then realized he was thinking this had to do with her visit to Sheridan. "No, um, no. This is different." She wiped her cheeks dry. "Why are you here?"

"You didn't come down to dinner."

"Oh no. It's six already?"

"Six fifteen." He grimaced. "You know how Dot is."

"Is she upset?"

"Just worried. She thought you might need help."

Briar turned away, hiding her face. "I do," she said, choking back a sob, "but not like you think."

"Let me tell Miss Warner you won't be coming down to dinner—unless you want to come down?"

She shook her head.

"Then I'll pass on the message and come right back and then maybe you'll tell me what's going on."

"Don't you want to keep her company?"

"Miss Warner is fine. I even suspect she'd enjoy a quiet night. She had some friends stop by this afternoon and they had fun catching up, but they were here for hours and she's a little worn out."

Jet was back in less than five minutes and Briar was calmer when he returned but that was only because she'd cried herself out.

She gestured to the chair by the window, but he shook

his head. "You sit. I'll listen."

Suddenly, she didn't know what she was supposed to say. She didn't know how to say it. Briar sat on the edge of her bed and stared toward the window. Thanks to the time change, it was still light and the trees outside were budding green. The hillsides were green as well. "I don't know where to start."

"How about with the real reason you're here?"

She turned and looked at him. "What does that mean?"

He grabbed the ottoman, dragged it forward and sat down in front of her. "I don't believe you're here because you had a hankering to work on the ranch or spend more time with Cade. You and Cade don't have an easy relationship and I appreciate that you want to get to know him better, but why now? What was so urgent you didn't call him first and ask if he wanted you here, or if he'd even be here? It's almost as if you made a mad dash for the border and here you are, hiding out."

She started to protest that she wasn't hiding out but then swallowed the protest and pressed her lips together. She was hiding. She was hiding from the world, hiding the truth, hiding from a future she couldn't yet face. "I don't know what to do."

Jet's intense gaze searched hers. "What's happened?"

There was no judgment in his voice, just a quiet authority that made her feel such a rush of confusing emotions. She craved peace. She craved security. She craved feeling safe.

What would happen when the truth came out? What would happen to her, and what would happen to her baby?

"Can I trust you?" she asked, voice pitched low.

Again, he just looked at her, his eyes piercing, as if looking all the way into her soul. "Always."

Always. It was the best answer possible, and yet it just made her feel worse. "I'm pregnant and I don't know what to do."

He didn't miss a beat. "How far along are you?"

"Twenty-eight weeks." She saw the flicker of surprise in his eyes. "I'm carrying small."

"When you say you don't know what to do, Briar, I think that means *you* know what you want to do, but you're not sure anyone else would approve."

He was one hundred percent correct. It was almost funny except she couldn't smile. She couldn't even cry. There were no tears left.

She left the bed and went to the chair where she'd been sitting filling out the paperwork and carried it to him. "I'm considering adoption. It's what I should do, at any rate."

He took the paperwork from her and scanned the front page and then the second. "Why this agency?"

"They do open adoptions. I could pick the couple, meet them, make sure I like the family who would raise her."

Jet's head lifted and his eyes met hers. "It's a girl?"

"Found out today. Had no idea." She struggled to keep her voice steady. "I wish I hadn't found out though. It makes it harder to do this ... give her away."

"Was that your plan when you came here?"

"I think so. But I've been torn from the beginning, which is why I wanted to talk to Cade. One thought was, I could stay here until I had the baby and then place the baby for adoption. My dad wouldn't need to know. His church members wouldn't know. No one in our community would know. Cade and MerriBee would know, but I hoped they'd be ... supportive. It even crossed my mind maybe he and MerriBee would want to adopt my baby. Not sure that's an option, though, but it's something I've considered."

Jet said nothing and she held her breath, her heart tender, her lungs aching.

"The other thought was, I'd stay here until I had the baby, and then I'd ... keep ... the baby. The problem is, I don't know how I'd make it without help, and I don't know if Cade will help."

"What about your dad?"

"I don't want to involve him."

"Why? I can't imagine he'd disown you."

"No, but he'd be deeply disappointed and with him being a man of God, he should be living a life above reproach." She wrinkled her nose. "I don't want to be the reproach. I've played the part for far too long."

Jet thought for a minute. "Cade isn't as hard as you think. He loves you very much and wants to protect you."

"Yes, but he has this idea of who I am, or who I should

be, and he doesn't realize it's too late for that. I'm not this innocent kid sister. I'm not a good little virgin—" She broke off, unable to finish. "I've made myself sick over this. Before I came here, I couldn't eat or sleep. I cried all the time, and it's been good for me being here without him here. Miss Warner is so inspiring. I feel so much stronger just knowing her. But this afternoon, when I began filling out the paperwork, I hurt so much I couldn't breathe."

"Does the baby's father know?" Jet asked.

She shook her head. "We're not in a relationship. It was a one and done, or you could say, won and done. Once he had what he wanted he was out of there."

"But you know who he is? You could find him if you wanted to?"

"I'm sure I could. He's in the public eye, competes on the rodeo circuit. But I don't want to find him. I don't ever want to see him again. It was a humiliating experience and I've no desire to relive any of it."

"But you're having his baby."

"*No.*" Briar had just sat back down but she shot to her feet. "She's not his baby. She's mine."

Jet didn't speak for a good minute, and the silence was nearly unbearable. "If she's yours," he said slowly, looking up at her, "why would you place her up for adoption?"

Briar's eyes burned and her stomach hurt, as if she'd swallowed a cup of nails. "I don't want to, but I have to consider all options. That's what a good mother would do. I can't be selfish. I can't just think of me."

His expression shifted, easing, sympathy in his eyes. "It's not selfish to want your own baby. It's not selfish to love your baby. That's what good mothers do."

She looked away and knocked away a tear before it could fall. "I was so scared I was going to lose her. So scared something was wrong with her. But there's nothing wrong. She's perfect."

"That's really good news."

Briar nodded and wiped her eyes again. "Cade isn't going to think this is good news."

"You're right. He's not going to be very open-minded, but that doesn't mean he won't get over it and be supportive."

"He says I'm like our mom. It's not a compliment, either." Briar's chest burned and ached. She was so tired of the pain and guilt. So tired of feeling as if she'd failed everyone. "I never knew her, but he's allowed to hold her mistakes over my head and judge me." Her voice hardened, and she knew she sounded bitter. "I don't even care that it's not fair. But I do care about what's going to happen next, as well as what's the best thing for the baby. Because she's what matters now."

"Yes," Jet said. "She matters. But you still matter. Can't you both be important at the same time?"

Briar began to pace the room, torn between relief that she'd finally shared the truth with someone, but also regret, because it wasn't her secret anymore. She couldn't control the story. She couldn't control how others would respond. "Why aren't you appalled?" she asked, turning at the window to face Jet.

"Because babies are miracles. You've made a life. And as upsetting as all of this is now, it's not the end of the world. In fact, it's just the beginning."

And then he completely shocked her by standing and crossing to her and wrapping his arms around her in a hug. "It's going to be okay," he said quietly. "*You're* going to be okay."

She clung to him for a moment, feeling as if she'd been thrown a lifeline. "Nothing will ever be the same."

He eased away from her, his hands on her shoulders. "That's true. But maybe things will be better. Maybe you'll be happier."

"How?"

"You've made a little human being, someone who will look to you for love and acceptance. Someone who will think you're the greatest person on the planet. Your baby comes into the world with unconditional love. All you have to do is return that love, and do your best to make good decisions for—"

He was interrupted by a rap on the door. Briar looked at Jet.

Jet whispered, "Breathe," and went to the door, opening it for her.

Miss Warner was there on the threshold. She glanced at

Jet and then Briar and then back to Jet. "So, this is where the party is," she said, a hint of a smile in her eyes.

Briar, who'd been wound so tight, started to laugh. She came to the door and hugged Miss Warner. "You are really funny, you know."

Miss Warner gestured down the hall. "It's a long walk here. I don't know why Emma put you as far from me as possible."

"I think to keep me from bothering you," Briar said, smiling and wiping away tears at the same time.

"Hmm. Not sure she succeeded. Now," she added, glancing again at Jet, "have you two sorted everything out? I don't mean to be rude, but I find lovers' quarrels exhausting."

Briar looked at Jet and he grinned at her and suddenly they were all going in different directions but out in the hall. Jet paused, caught her eye again, and then walked on, escorting Miss Warner back to her wing.

Briar closed the door gently, not sure whether to laugh or cry. Lovers' quarrel indeed.

Chapter Six

For the first time in a long time Briar felt almost calm. As if things would be okay. As if she'd be okay. Nothing had changed, no decision had been made, but she felt peace.

Her heart didn't ache and burn. She didn't feel like the worst human being.

It helped that Jet hadn't been judgmental. He hadn't asked questions—other than about the father of her child—that made her feel as if she was too young and too irresponsible.

She appreciated how he'd been thoughtful and respectful. He'd treated her as if she was intelligent, and capable, and that confidence in her made her hope. Believe.

She would have never guessed that Jet would be the one to give her hope, or relief. She would have never dreamed Jet would be the ally she'd needed.

Briar still didn't have all the answers—but she had some. She could finally admit she wanted her baby. She did want to keep her daughter and raise her. The particulars were still overwhelming but at least Briar had a direction and a goal—to figure out how she could keep her baby and give her daughter the life she deserved.

Downstairs, Briar found Emma back in the kitchen, humming happily as she mixed up pancake batter and fried bacon. Emma was excited that Willis was returning tonight. Cade and his family would be back soon, too. Today, tomorrow, or the day after.

Seeing Cade made her nervous, though.

"Anything exciting happen this week while I was lounging in bed?" Emma asked, turning the bacon.

Briar smiled faintly. "I wouldn't say you were lounging. But no, you missed nothing. Just glad things are getting back to normal."

"I'm glad, too. I missed Willis more than I expected. It was hard with him gone that long."

"Why didn't you go with him?" Briar asked, leaning over to steal a strawberry from Miss Warner's fruit bowl.

"I hate leaving Miss Warner. She's like my family, now, and I worry when away from her."

"Do you think you'd feel that way even if you and Willis had kids?"

"Oh yes. Family isn't just those that share your DNA. Family are the people that treat you well, the people who want the best for you, and give you what you need. I've always thought it strange that there are so many families which are broken and members are estranged. I always thought family would be the people that love you and forgive you, but somehow in our society, it doesn't always work that way. Maybe it's a good thing that marriage allows you to choose your family. I'm so lucky Willis became mine."

"I'm looking forward to seeing him again," Briar answered. "I don't remember him very well from my first visit here."

"It was a rushed visit," Emma said. "We were all so happy you had found Cade—he'd been trying to find you for years—but then it wasn't an easy time for either of you. I know MerriBee was just beside herself. Cade can be tough, he's been through a lot, but he's so sweet with MerriBee and Grace, and it was a little shocking to see how hard he was on you."

Briar shrugged. "I wasn't the sister he'd imagined. I think he was shocked and disappointed."

"No." Emma used tongs to lift the crispy bacon to a paper towel before draining the fat into a ceramic jar. "He was not disappointed. How could you even think that?" she said, placing the still hot skillet on a back burner.

Briar's chest suddenly grew tender, and her throat ached. "I could tell. And I know when he's back, it's going to get messy. I'd hoped to stay here through the summer, but it might not be possible."

"Yes, this is Cade's ranch now, but it's also still Miss Warner's. Miss Warner likes having you here. She enjoys your company, and because you're staying in the house, too, not in Cade's cabin, I don't think Cade can kick you out—" Emma broke off and held up a finger. "Have you seen the photo of Cade and your mom? Miss Warner took it when Cade brought his mom here for a visit during his first summer working at the Sundowner. Cade was proud of being part of the staff and he wanted his mom to see where he worked."

"I haven't seen it. I asked Cade if he had any photos of our mom and he said they were all put away."

"Well, this one's in the library. Come, I'll show you."

Emma led the way into the library, and she scanned the room with its floor-to-ceiling bookshelves before walking to one bookshelf that had some framed photos in front of the leather-bound volumes. She picked up the cloisonné frame and handed it to Briar. "It's a little faded but you'll see why Cade can't help but adore you. You look so very much like your mom."

Briar looked at the photo of Cade and Suzy taken outside with a line of tethered horses behind them. Sunlight gilded them and Cade's hair was long and bleached blond from the sun. Suzy was smaller, the top of her head barely reaching Cade's shoulder. She was wearing a jean jacket and she had a slim frame, dark brown hair, and light eyes fringed with long black lashes. From the photo, it was hard to tell what color her eyes were, but it didn't matter. Suzy had Briar's face. Or Briar had Suzy's face. The cheekbones, the same nose, the same mouth, the same chin.

"I think this was just before your mom was diagnosed with cancer. It's why she was so thin."

Briar couldn't look away from the image. Even young, Cade's expression was set, his mouth pressed thin. He looked uncomfortable—or was it uneasy?—but at the same time he stood with his arm around his mom's shoulders, and his posture felt protective, whereas Suzy just looked proud. You could almost feel her pride through the photo as she smiled at the camera.

They had a complicated relationship, Briar thought, which was maybe why she and Cade had a complicated relationship as well.

He felt protective of his mom but in the end, he couldn't save her.

He felt protective of his sister but didn't know how to protect her.

Briar put the photo back on the shelf. "Thank you for sharing that with me. Cade had said I looked like Mom, but I didn't realize until now how much we do."

BRIAR HAD RETURNED to the library after breakfast to look once more at the photo of Cade and their mom, and it was only when Briar was holding the photo the second time she realized she had already been born when this picture had been taken. In fact, if Cade was sixteen then she would have been three.

Briar didn't remember being three, but she remembered photos her parents had of her at three. The third birthday party. The little denim embroidered dress and red felt hat and cowboy boots. Fergus, the black-and-white border collie, at her side. She hadn't thought about Fergus in years, but he'd been a great dog, so attentive she used to get mad at him because he wouldn't let her run away.

Briar put the framed photo back. She'd really had an idyllic childhood. From the moment she'd been born she'd been surrounded by love. With so much on her mind, she craved exercise and fresh air and went for a walk, circling around the ranch house and passing some of the young cowboys setting off on their ATVs. Rolly was one of them, but she didn't know the name of the other. But they waved to her, and she smiled and then on impulse she drew out her phone and called her brother. He answered, which surprised her. Or maybe it shouldn't surprise her.

"Hi, Cade, just thought I'd check in and see how you're all doing," she said when he answered.

"Better. MerriBee is starting to bounce back. We should be home this weekend."

"That's good."

"How has it been at the house? Surviving okay?"

"I actually really like it. Emma is awesome and Miss Warner and I get along really well.

We watch *Wheel of Fortune* and *Jeopardy* and have ice cream or whatever Emma has baked."

"I used to do that with Dot. She knows most of the answers, have you noticed that?"

"I have. She's pretty impressive."

"Well, thank you for spending so much time with her. I appreciate it more than you know."

For a second Briar couldn't speak. "It's not a hardship, Cade, it's a privilege. I never had a grandmother. I just feel lucky that Miss Warner opened her home to me."

When Briar finally returned to the kitchen to help with lunch and dinner prep, she found Jet there, unpacking a box of flour and sugars and other pantry staples and then putting them away at Emma's direction.

While Emma and Jet chatted, mostly about Willis's trip to San Diego, Briar glanced at the recipe card lying on the counter. It looked like they'd be having beef burgundy tonight. Briar scanned the recipe noting the vegetables to be chopped. She began gathering the onions and carrots when Emma paused to tell her they'd be tripling the recipe. Briar gathered more onions and carrots and took up her place at the counter where she always did her work.

After peeling the onions, Briar began dicing both the onions and carrots, and she'd never say it out loud, but she felt rather proud of herself for how quickly she could do it now. When she first arrived at the ranch it had taken forever to chop something. Now, she knew how to hold the knife and position the vegetables and get things done faster, with less effort and anxiety, and wasn't that also a good lesson in life?

Practice mattered, but you didn't gain experience without putting in the effort.

The kitchen intercom came on and it was Miss Warner requesting Emma's assistance. Emma bustled out leaving Briar and Jet together. For a moment, neither said anything to each other and then Briar glanced at Jet, noting his handsome profile.

"Were you able to get any sleep?" Jet asked gruffly.

"Yes. Probably my best night in a long time."

"It's a lot to carry by yourself. I'm surprised you haven't told anyone."

"Well, I did tell MerriBee earlier in the week, when I needed to see a doctor."

Jet leaned against the counter, his thumbs hooked over his belt. "Other than get you into a doctor, was there any conversation?"

Briar shook her head.

"I'm surprised," Jet said. "I would have thought she'd want to talk to you."

"I think she was respecting my privacy, figuring we'd talk when I was ready, which was probably when they came home."

"They're coming home tonight, aren't they?"

"I just talked to him, and I think they'll try tomorrow. Depends if MerriBee's up to it."

"She got it, too?"

"Sounds like it."

Jet grimaced. "I don't want it."

"Me, either." Briar leaned toward him and whispered,

"Do you think we could suggest they stay away for another week?"

Jet flashed a white smile, making him even more devastatingly handsome. "No, but I'm with you." After a moment his smile faded. "I owe you an apology. I didn't sleep very well. I was worried about you, and I hated to think that all this time you've been keeping this a secret, that you've had no one to talk to, or share with. I'm really sorry."

"It's not your fault. You didn't get me into this situation."

"But I could have been a better friend to you, especially that night when you came by the bunkhouse—"

"It's okay," she said quickly, cutting him short. "It's not important. I was having a hard night, but that's not your problem. I'm not your problem and, honestly, you were smart to send me on my way. I might have got us in trouble that night. I craved company." *I craved you.*

"Can we be friends now?" he asked. "I'd like to be someone you felt safe with. Someone you could trust."

She glanced through the kitchen opening into the dining room but there was no sign of Emma, no sign of anyone. She turned back to Jet, a hint of urgency in her voice. "Do you think I'm crazy to want to keep my baby?"

"No," he said firmly. "I don't think you're crazy at all."

"Do you think I could be a good mom? Most people would say I'm not exactly a role model of responsibility."

"Most people don't know you."

"Cade—"

"Doesn't know you." Jet's gaze met hers and held. "You're a very responsible person, especially when you want to be."

"Isn't everybody."

"Not necessarily. So let me ask you a few questions. You have a horse, yes?"

Briar frowned. "I know where you're going with this, but you can't possibly compare a baby to a horse."

He grinned. "For the sake of this discussion, yes. Now bear with me. You have a horse."

Briar sighed. "Yes."

"You take excellent care of Judas."

She suddenly wished she'd named her horse something else. Just one more reminder of her rebellious self. "Yes."

"Why?"

"Because I do. I love him."

"You don't forget to feed him," Jet added.

"No, never."

"You stable him at night, you make sure he's warm. If he's sick you call the vet."

"Of course."

"Why would you be any different with a baby?"

The lump returned, filling her throat, making her chest ache. But what if there were others who could be a better mother? Wasn't that something she had to think about as well?

A good mother did what was best for the child. A truly loving mother would sacrifice for her child, and Briar believed her daughter deserved the world, not instability and financial insecurity.

It would all be so much different if she was older and had a proper job. If she were more settled, she'd fight to keep the baby because she wanted her little girl. There was no confusion there. She loved her child, and that love made her willing to make impossible decisions, decisions that would break her heart.

"I think you're the only one who thinks this way," Briar said, voice cracking. "Everyone else will call me reckless and irresponsible—"

"Maybe, and maybe not. But why do you care what others think? What's important is how you view yourself. Only you know your true self-worth, and only you know your strength. If you want your child, you can do it. Will it be easy? No. Will you struggle? Yes. But would it be worth it? That's for you to answer, and only you."

With a brisk step, Emma entered the kitchen and brightened when she saw Jet still there. "Oh, Jet dear, can you do me a huge favor? Miss Warner is moving one of her paintings and I'd thought I could help her but it's just too heavy for me. Would you mind seeing what you could do?"

"Of course," Jet said to her, before looking at Briar. "We can talk later if you want."

She nodded. "I want."

AN HOUR LATER Briar got a text from Jet. *I forgot the eggs. Want to make a grocery store run with me? We could get some ice cream.*

Ice cream? Escape the ranch? See Jet? *Yes,* she texted immediately. *When?*

Leaving now. I'll swing by the house and pick you up.

Briar grabbed her coat and purse, stopped by Emma's apartment to let her know she was heading to Story with Jet and asked if there was anything else she needed.

"I think Jet has the list," Emma said.

"Okay." Briar blew her a kiss and raced out to find Jet's truck already parked out front.

The first part of the ride Briar just relaxed, happy that Jet had rolled the truck windows down and the fresh air was blowing through. She pulled the elastic off her ponytail and let her hair free and breathed in deeply, feeling almost as free. How good it was to not feel so overwhelmed and alone. She'd needed a friend desperately and who would have thought Jet Manning would become that person?

She glanced at him, and his lovely blue eyes met hers. His skin was tanned and there were creases at the corners of his eyes. She would never call them laugh lines, he wasn't one to laugh easily, but it was a face she found impossibly appealing.

"You look happy," he said, returning his focus to the narrow ranch road that wound down the mountain to the highway.

She thought about it for a moment. "I am happy. Maybe happier than I have a right to be."

"Impossible. Happiness is essential to the quality of one's life."

"Hmm. Are you happy?"

He made a rough sound. "We're not talking about me."

"Why not? You are just as important as anyone else. Why shouldn't you be happy?"

"Because I would have made different choices if happiness was my main concern." He extended an arm outside his window, fingers wide, letting the air pass through.

She was more intrigued than ever. "So, what was your main concern?"

"Revenge."

She sat forward. "Really?"

"Yes, and that choice changed everything." He glanced at her, expression inscrutable. "It was an ugly, brutal choice but it was the only choice I had—despite the consequences."

"What did you do?"

"It doesn't matter now. What's done is done. I've made a new life for me and it's working out."

"Is your new life here on the Sundowner?"

"Yes."

"What did you do before … if you don't mind me asking?"

He hesitated a moment. "I was a fighter pilot, for the US

Navy."

Her jaw dropped and she gave her head the smallest of shakes unable to process what he'd just said. A fighter pilot? "Like Maverick in *Top Gun?*"

"Yeah."

She rubbed her face, pressing her fingers against her forehead and eyes as if that could help her think more clearly.

He cast her a cynical smile. "Surprised?"

"*Yes.*" Briar exhaled, still trying to take it all in. "Why did you quit?"

"I didn't. I was thrown out as a consequence for my mistake."

"So, what did you do?"

"Aggravated assault, which is a felony. Unfortunately, the Navy's top brass frowns on that sort of thing and don't want their officers associated with felons and violent offenders so there went my career."

Briar just stared at him.

Her shock seemed to amuse him. "You seem very surprised."

"I *am*. You are so controlled. You're so careful about everything ... I can't believe you're, you know..."

"A felon?"

She nodded.

"Sorry, sweets. Now you know why your brother doesn't want you near me. I'm not good boyfriend material, nor the kind of man you bring home to meet Dad." He gave her a meaningful look. "Especially your dad."

They drove the rest of the way to Story in silence. It wasn't an uncomfortable silence, but thoughtful more than anything.

Briar was truly caught off guard. Jet didn't seem like a violent offender. He didn't seem abusive or dangerous. As Jet found a spot on Main near the small market where they'd get the eggs and cream Emma wanted, Briar saw a small clothing store across the street and asked Jet if he'd mind if she popped in.

"No," he said. "Go ahead. I'll meet you there."

She entered the small store and realized almost right away she wouldn't find what she needed, but she studied the sweaters and extra-large shirts hoping something might work. Jet joined her a few minutes later and watched her go through the two racks of women's clothing. "What are you looking for?" he asked.

She blushed. "I've nearly outgrown everything I own. I could use a few maternity tops, and if I could find it, one pair of jeans." She didn't mention the need for a new bra, but she'd love one of those if possible, too.

He glanced around the store. "Nothing here though?"

"No." Briar pulled out her phone and did a quick search. "There is a maternity store on Main Street in Sheridan, but that's another half hour away. Not sure we can be gone that long today."

"Why not? Emma's back at the helm. Willis is back tonight, in fact, he should be landing soon—"

"Do we need to get him?"

"No, his truck is at the Billings airport. He might even beat us home. So, honestly, it's a good time to go, and we can be back at the Sundowners in a little over ninety minutes if we skip the ice cream."

"Let's skip the ice cream. I need jeans that fit."

JET WAS IMPRESSED by the speed Briar shopped. He waited in the truck while she shopped but less than ten minutes after she'd gone in, she came out, showing him two shirts, one a white T-shirt that she said, *should grow with her*, and a long-sleeve denim blouse that was made for pregnant bellies, along with the pair of jeans she wanted.

"That was incredibly impressive," he said. "Did you get everything you wanted?"

"Everything I thought necessary. Maternity clothes are expensive and I'm not going to be pregnant forever, so I didn't want to spend much."

"If you need money—"

"No!" she exclaimed. "I have a little money, and this isn't your problem. I'm not your problem."

"Could I at least treat you to ice cream? Well, it's frozen yogurt, but there's a store right across the street. We could grab it and go."

"Yes. I love frozen yogurt, even more than ice cream because of all the toppings."

"What kind do you get?"

"Favorite would be vanilla and cake batter, with those pink and white frosted animal cracker cookies on top. The more the better."

"Let's hope they have them."

They were the only customers in the frozen yogurt shop on a late March afternoon at almost two o'clock. The boy behind the counter said they could try as many flavors as they wanted, and Briar tried three before picking her favorite, cake batter, covering it with the pink and white frosted cookies she liked. As they walked back to his truck, he was pretty sure she was skipping, and as she took bites, she made little yum-yum noises that made him smile.

It was good to see her smiling, especially after last night when she'd been so broken. It killed him seeing her like that—desperate, devastated. Ashamed. She shouldn't be alone with this; she was only half of the equation. So where was the other half? Why wasn't he involved, supportive? Why wasn't he feeling the burden as much as she was?

It ticked Jet off that society always put the majority of the blame on the woman when a pregnancy couldn't happen without two. Just because the man could walk away didn't mean he should.

As if reading his mind, Briar turned to him inside the truck. "Do you think I have to tell the person who fathered my baby?"

Jet searched her eyes. "Are we talking morally, ethically, legally?"

"Aren't morally and ethically the same thing?"

"They both distinguish between right and wrong, but ethically tends to be a community or society measurement, whereas morally is a personal measurement. So, what would society say—ethics. What you personally feel—your morality."

She was quiet for a moment as he started the car and began driving.

"Well then, morally, no, I don't think he deserves to know. Ethically, yes, every father should know. And legally ... I think he has a legal right, and responsibility, to his child. But will he accept it? Knowing Garrett, I think not. But maybe that's wishful thinking since I want nothing to do with him."

Jet glanced at her as he merged onto the highway south. "But he should know, right?"

Briar gave him a look that made it clear she didn't agree before returning her attention to her cup of frozen yogurt.

Chapter Seven

B RIAR GOT THROUGH dinner and television time without betraying any of her inner turmoil, but once Miss Warner had gone to her room, Briar left the house and walked down to the barn and texted Jet on the way. *Do you really think I should tell Garrett?*

Yes. The answer came immediately. *Then at least you know where he stands. I believe it's always important to get your facts before making an important decision.*

She exhaled and slid her phone in her back pocket. She was wearing the new jeans, so much more comfortable with the stretchy waistband and the stretchy denim fabric piece built into the tummy portion.

"Hey," Jet's voice sounded in the dark. "Where are you going?"

She slowed and scanned the bunkhouse, and then saw him sitting on the front steps. "I'm going to hang out in the barn and get some equine therapy."

"I'll join you," he said, standing up. "Unless you'd rather I not?"

"No, come. The more the merrier. Maybe we can make this a weekly thing. Horses and Friends every Thursday at eight o'clock."

His teeth gleamed in the dark. "I have a feeling you'd like that."

"I'd far rather meet with horses weekly than people. I tolerate people. I love horses."

He held open the door for her as they reached the barn. A dozen heads appeared over the stall doors, the horses all different colors. Briar smiled, already feeling less troubled. "Aren't they gorgeous?"

"I wasn't raised with horses, but I've come to appreciate them."

"But you have no horse of your own? There's not one you feel a special bond with?"

"When I first arrived, I bonded with Traitor Joe—"

"Wait, what? Traitor Joe or Trader Joe's?" she asked, sitting down on one of the hay bales in the corner and leaning against the wall.

He took a seat on another, stretched his legs out. "Traitor Joe. Despite his name, he and I had a really good rapport. No one else liked him, but he was kind of my boy."

"What happened to him?"

"Apparently he'd only been on loan here and so six months after I arrived, he and a half dozen horses were returned to another dude ranch in Idaho."

"I didn't know that was a thing."

"It seems a number of the dude ranches will move horses from one place to another, depending on the ranch's summer needs."

"I bet you could buy him back," she said.

"It's okay, I make do with what's here."

"You're not a very good horse owner."

He laughed at her indignant expression. "You're a little ridiculous."

"Horses have feelings. They're very sensitive."

"They're also working animals and highly adaptable. Treat them well and they'll bond with the next person that gives them pats and treats. For example, your Judas—"

"Don't," she interrupted, holding up her hand. "Don't even joke about wooing away Judas. That's my baby. Well"—she put a hand to her belly—"one of my babies." For a moment neither of them spoke, and then she broke the silence, asking, "Would you go with me if I were to go tell Garrett about the baby? You don't need to be in the room, but I'd feel better if you were nearby. Just in case."

Jet's gaze narrowed. "In case what?"

She shrugged. "In case I lose courage. In case I cry. In case ... I don't know. But I'm nervous and scared." Briar cleared her throat. "I don't get scared very often but this is not going to be easy."

"I get that. But it is the right thing to do. And for what it's worth, I'm proud of you."

"That's a first," she said trying to joke, but the words came out on a husky note.

"Not true. If you had a fan club, I'd join and I'd definitely sign up for your newsletter."

Briar giggled, and then her laughter faded. "Could we do it this weekend? It would be a drive. Garrett is going to be in Fort Collins this weekend for a rodeo. I don't have his phone number so I can't call him. But then, it probably is better to break the news face-to-face."

"Fort Collins isn't a bad drive. I've done it before with Willis. It's around five, five and a half hours each way from here. We did a roundtrip comfortably in one day."

"I wouldn't say eleven hours in a truck is the most comfortable way to spend a day, but I'm really grateful you'll keep me company. Should I drive?"

"Do you want to drive?"

"Not necessarily but if you would prefer being the passenger—"

"No. I much prefer driving. I love driving. I love speed and control."

"That's right. You were a pilot."

Jet didn't lose his smile, but she saw the light die in his eyes. She felt his pain. Briar swallowed around the lump in her throat. "Did you like being a pilot?" she asked softly.

"Loved it."

"Is that what you always wanted to be?"

"No," he said. "It was the backup career plan. My dream was to be an astronaut, but it wasn't going to work out, so I found another career path and I liked it, a lot."

Jet's phone vibrated, and then Briar's. Briar looked at her

messages first. "It's MerriBee," she said. "She texted to say they're on their way."

Jet put away his phone. "My message was from Cade. They should be here soon. They're just passing Story now."

Briar's stomach flip-flopped and she exhaled hard. "I dread this," she said lowly. "I'm so afraid to tell him."

"Your brother, or Garrett?" Jet said, rising and giving her a hand, gently pulling her to her feet.

"Both," Briar answered. She glanced down her body, patted her vest covered shirt. "Do I look pregnant?"

Jet scrutinized her then shook his head. "No. You hide it well, but you probably won't be able to do that much longer."

"I guess it's good I'll talk to Garrett this weekend. At least I'll know what he's thinking."

"And I'll know my schedule better after I talk to Cade," Jet said. "How about we firm our plans tomorrow night?"

"Sounds good. Now I'm going to head to bed."

"You don't want to wait for Cade?" he teased.

"No. I need sleep, and then some tea—" She broke off as her phone buzzed again. She checked the new text and then smiled, relieved. "That was Cade," she said, texting Cade back. "He said they're all tired from a long day on the road and hoped I would be okay catching up in the morning."

"And what did you say?"

She grinned. "That I'll see him in the morning."

CADE WAS UP at the main house at eight to have breakfast with Miss Warner. Miss Warner was clearly happy to see him, and they spent breakfast catching up and discussing what Miss Warner seemed most interested in lately—hay and alfalfa.

It was nine when Miss Warner disappeared into her library to read her books and magazines and agricultural business reports. Instead of leaving, Cade sought Briar out and asked her to take a walk with him so they could talk while he got ready to start his day.

"Dot looks good," he said to Briar. "I was concerned about being away so long, but you've taken excellent care of her."

"I haven't done anything, and just an FYI, Miss Warner still thinks she's the boss here."

"She is," he answered. "This is, and will always be, the Warner family ranch."

"So why has she giving it to you?"

"Because she's made me family. She knows I'll take care of this place the way she would, and I'll remember her the way she deserves."

The sincerity of his answer made her heart hurt a little. "She's pretty amazing. When I think about what she's done, and had to do, when most women her age had very little authority, never mind, autonomy, it's so impressive. And she doesn't sound as if she wants to retire from managing the ranch anytime soon. It sounds like she wants to get another property as well. She and Jet have talked a lot about buying a farm and growing alfalfa."

"How did you know?"

"She's had Jet up for dinner, and one evening they talked an hour straight about best hay practices." Briar rolled her eyes. "It was very boring after a bit, but then, I don't understand hay. Now you might have loved it."

Cade's brow furrowed, apparently hearing only one thing. "She had Jet up for dinner?"

"Now and then, when she wanted to discuss business." Briar looked up at him. "Is that a problem?"

"No, I'm just ... surprised. She didn't need to have him for dinner to discuss business. She usually does that during lunch, or a meeting during the day."

Briar shrugged. "I don't know the whys. Does it bother you?"

"Dot has always kept a fairly deep line between staff and family."

"But you made the jump to family."

"And apparently you have, too," he said, tweaking her nose a little. His gaze dropped and he scanned her frame. "You look good," he said, "not quite so thin. How are you feeling?"

"Good." She smiled at him, ignoring the niggling worry that she looked big, and he'd figure out what was going on before she could tell him. "And Dot kind of feels like the grandmother I never had. Now, don't tell her that, but I really do love spending time with her."

LATE THAT AFTERNOON, Jet entered the kitchen carrying a box. "Chicken thighs, pork chops and ground beef," he said, placing the box on the counter. "Emma, should any of this go in the freezer or do you want it all in the outdoor fridge?"

She peeked into the box, removed the pork chops, all six packages, and then said the rest could go in the refrigerator.

"And I can do that," Briar said, reaching for the box. "I'm sure you have a lot to do now that Cade is home."

"It's on the heavy side," Jet said. "I'd feel better taking care of it. But you could open the door for me if you don't mind?"

Briar tried not to smile, hoping he didn't know how happy she was to see him. She'd gotten used to seeing him every day, early in the day, but with Cade back, everyone was busy.

"How is your day going?" she asked him, leading the way into the mudroom where she opened the built-in refrigerator's huge door.

"Good," he said. "And it's better now, seeing you. You look pretty in red."

She glanced down, patted her sternum where she'd buttoned the first button on the red plaid flannel shirt. "It's Willis's shirt," she said, watching as Jet filled the refrigerator with an incredible amount of meat. "He brought back a lot of new clothes from California, so Emma made him get rid of a few. This is one of the castoffs. I snagged it before she sent the paper bag down to the bunkhouse."

"So that's where those shirts came from," Jet said closing the door and then going to the mudroom sink to wash his hands.

"Did you take any?"

"No, they were all too small for me."

"Oh, right. You have so many muscles."

Jet flicked a little water at her. "Smart-ass."

She laughed and spun away, her pulse racing, butterflies flitting in her middle. It wasn't the first time Jet gave her serious butterflies. But it was the first time it crossed her mind that she was falling for him, and she didn't even want to think what that meant. It just felt good to feel something good. She'd felt so bad about herself for far too long.

Jet winked at her and headed out through the mudroom to the yard. As the door closed behind him Briar smiled, feeling fizzy and hopeful—

"Ahem."

Briar turned sharply and discovered Cade in the doorway between the mudroom and kitchen. She froze, going hot and then cold. She had no idea how long Cade had been standing there. "Hi," she said, smiling at him trying to cover her nerves.

"Hello," he said almost toneless. "Could we talk?"

She thought they'd talked earlier, but of course they

could talk again. "Sure. Do you want to talk in here, or go somewhere else?"

"Let's go to the dining room. It should be quiet in there."

It was a brief but uncomfortable walk through the kitchen, past Emma, to the dining room. Briar sat down in a chair and waited, hands in her lap, while Cade took a seat. She could tell from Cade's eyes that he was troubled by something. Troubled by her? But she hadn't done anything wrong.

"You seem upset," she said, trying not to be anxious but it was hard to be around him.

"Upset isn't the right word. Concerned is more like it. I'm concerned about the situation here—"

"Me being here?"

"No, but about Jet, and the ranch. Stop me if Dot has already told you about the program here."

"I take it you're not talking about the summer dude ranch program."

He shook his head. "We run a program on the Sundowner for men who need second chances." Cade's gaze met hers and held. "It's for men who might find it difficult to get hired somewhere else. They work here for a year or two, and then move on to something else, something they're more passionate about. Sometimes, they come back because this is what they want to do, and other times we never see them again, but in general, the ranch is a good place for them while they get their act together."

Suddenly things began to make sense to her. All the times Cade warned her away from the bunkhouse. The references to the cowboys, and specifically about Jet, not needing trouble.

"Is Jet one of those men?" she asked.

"I don't discuss any of the men's personal situations—"

"But is Jet someone you worry about?" she interrupted. "Do you trust him?"

"Yes."

"Does Miss Warner?"

"What are you doing?" Cade asked, frustrated. "I'm trying to share something important with you and instead of listening you're asking questions."

"It's just that you've warned me away from him on more than one occasion. I just wondered if Jet had a dangerous history—" She broke off, remembering what Jet had told her. He had a criminal past. He had a felony, something assault. "Do you worry that Jet would hurt me?"

"He's not dangerous, nor violent, with women. He's protective of every person here. I respect him a great deal, but Briar, listen to me. He's not for you."

Briar held her breath and fought to keep her temper. "I don't really think that's for you to decide, Cade. I know you mean well, but I'm not a child."

"Briar, I'm not trying to push your buttons, and I hope you're not trying to push mine, but I'm letting you know right now, what I will and won't tolerate if you hope to remain on this ranch. I'm not going to have you pursued by a man a decade older than you."

"What if he's not doing the pursuing? What if I am?"

"No. And he knows you're off-limits, so there is that."

She'd been trying to be funny, but now she was serious. "But what about friends? Can we at least be friends?"

"As long as you're never alone together, and there's no private communication, then sure, be friends all you want."

Briar just stared at Cade.

"Be mad," Cade said. "This is in your best interest—"

"And does MerriBee agree? Have you discussed this with her?"

"Why would I discuss this with her?"

"Because she's your wife and a lot more in touch with reality than you are." Briar started to stand but Cade put his hand out on her arm and stopped her.

"Jet knows the rules. You know them, too. Don't test me, Briar. It won't work out the way you want things to. Jet needs this job. He needs his self-respect. Maybe you don't care what happens to you but have the decency to care about what happens to him." Cade rose abruptly and walked out of the dining room and let the front door slam closed behind him.

Briar didn't move. She sat, stunned, and numb.

A minute later Miss Warner appeared in the dining room doorway, her face creased with worry. "Was that Cade shouting?"

Briar nodded.

"I've never heard him raise his voice before," Miss Warner said, baffled.

"I pushed his buttons," Briar said unhappily.

"Should I ask what it's about?"

"No." Briar rubbed her face and straightened. "I'll try to talk to him later, but after he calms down. He's not going to listen to anything I have to say now."

"Can I ask what it is about?"

Briar hesitated and then nodded. "Jet. I'm not to have any communication with Jet unless there are others in the room."

Miss Warner sighed. "I see."

Chapter Eight

Sunday morning, they left the Sundowner at four forty-five. It was an hour earlier than they'd initially agreed, but when Briar reviewed the event schedule Saturday night, she was worried she might miss Garrett if she wasn't in Fort Collins by ten. Jet agreed and so they left earlier than planned, with a stop for coffee once they were on the highway as Jet couldn't drive without at least one large cup of strong black coffee.

It was good to be on the road. Briar had been nervous all night, worried that Cade would discover the plan and put a stop to it—not that he had any right to tell her where she could go, or with whom. But she loved her brother even if she didn't always understand him, and today was important. This meeting with Garrett was important and she could barely sip from her water bottle as her stomach churned.

It didn't help that she was happy to have this time with Jet. She felt guilty for being so happy, especially as it could blow up in their faces. But Cade was heading to outside Yellowstone today to meet a video photographer who was interested in documenting the Sundowner Ranch as well as

Miss Warner's role in it. Cade wasn't about to let the guy close to the ranch or Miss Warner until he'd thoroughly vetted him.

When they returned tonight, there might be some questions, but at that point Briar would maybe feel comfortable sharing her news with everyone. Possibly.

Unlikely.

She must have said something out loud because Jet glanced at her. "Did you just growl?" he asked.

"Maybe. I think I'm just really wound up."

"Not surprised. It's a big day."

And not just for the reasons he suspected. She was breathless for all the wrong reasons. She was too happy being here with Jet, just being with Jet. And in his truck in the early morning darkness, it felt as if they were the only ones in the universe. There were almost no other cars or trucks on the road and, although Jet's truck headlights created arrows of light, the morning still felt like a cocoon. It was just the two of them and she was aware of everything about him. His warmth, his big shoulders, his long legs, his muscular arm, and his hand as it rested on the steering wheel. He was wearing a thermal shirt, long sleeves, but they were pushed up on his forearms, revealing his wrists and taut tendons.

She swallowed hard, willing her attention to something else, preferably something outside, something not tall, dark, and handsome.

This was how she got in trouble in the first place. She

couldn't be a sucker for a gorgeous face. Or a big, gorgeous body.

Garrett had never given her butterflies. No one had ever given her butterflies. Just Jet.

It would be easier if she could ignore him ... or ignore the attraction.

"What if Garrett suggested marriage?" Jet asked, breaking the silence and glancing at her as he drove. "Would you consider it?"

Briar felt as if he'd doused her with cold water. Immediately, she shook her head. She didn't even have to think about it. "*No*. I couldn't marry him. I shouldn't have been with him the first time. I certainly won't spend the rest of my life with him. He's not a good person."

"What drew you to him in the first place?"

"He was good-looking."

"There you go."

But not like you, she thought, *he was nothing like you.*

"Where did you meet?" Jet asked.

"At Marietta's Copper Mountain Rodeo. I saw him at the street dance, not knowing he was there for the rodeo. He was having fun, and not every cowboy can dance, but he could. We danced, and had drinks, and danced some more..." She shook her head. "And then, you know."

Jet didn't say anything and, uncomfortable, she looked out her window. The sky had not yet started to lighten, and she felt the weight of the darkness, the heaviness of her mistakes, the disappointment, the shame. "I regret everything about that night. I wish I could have a redo and I wouldn't go into town that night. I wouldn't be anywhere near Marietta or the rodeo. I'd be home hanging out with Dad and taking care of things at the house. I could have cleaned or—"

"You were twenty-one, Briar," Jet interrupted. "You're allowed to go have fun."

"But not be stupid."

"How were you stupid?"

"I didn't—he didn't—use protection. And I knew I should say something, but I didn't."

Now Jet looked stunned. "Why not? You could get more than a baby by not insisting on a condom. You could get a disease you can't get rid of."

"I was trying to seem cool," she whispered.

"What?"

Her eyes felt dry and gritty, but she wasn't going to cry anymore. "I should have known better, but I didn't think you could really get pregnant your first time. But now I know."

Jet said nothing, but Briar saw how his fingers tightened around the steering wheel and from the set of his jaw it was obvious he was upset.

"But I know now," she added lightly, almost defiantly, because she wasn't about to let Jet make her feel bad, too. She had learned her lesson, and she'd lived with regret for twenty-eight weeks. There was nothing she could do about that night except make better decisions moving forward.

Jet took a deep breath. "I'm not mad at you, Briar. I want to kill *him*. I want to take his pathetic little—"

"No! No, Jet, you don't," she interrupted firmly, giving him an intentionally sorrowful look. "You have a criminal record. You'd get a life sentence for sure."

For a moment, Jet said nothing and then he laughed, laughing so hard tears came to his eyes. "You are ruthless."

"I've heard that before."

Jet laughed again. "You're also funny, and I like that."

"When I first met you, I didn't think you had a sense of humor."

"When I first met you, I thought you were incredibly spoiled."

"What?" She turned to look at him. "Why?"

He shrugged. "I know your dad, and let's face it, unless he's fooling us all, you've hit the lottery with him."

"Dad is exactly what he appears to be—solid, real, compassionate, giving. I did hit the jackpot with him. And I love him."

"So why not tell him about your pregnancy? Why keep the burden to yourself? Knowing him, he would always support you."

"He would. Dad would never throw me out, and he wouldn't tell me how disappointed he was. He wouldn't ever want me to feel shame, but he's going to be so disappointed.

He'll carry it on the inside, and he'll feel as if he failed, which isn't right since he didn't fail. I failed. I was the one who messed up and I'm not going to let him go through the rest of his life thinking he should have done something a little different. I don't want him praying, asking God for guidance because he has let me down, or asking God to forgive him for not being a better parent. My dad is a great dad, and if I keep my baby, he'll be a wonderful grandfather, but he's not going to be stuck with raising my baby. I'm not going to let him feel guilt or responsible for my mistakes. I'm going to figure this out and protect him. It's time I did that. It's the least I can do."

Jet reached over and took her hand. "No matter what decision you make, I want you to know I respect you and support you. I can't speak for your dad, but I am certain he would feel the same way."

"As long as he doesn't know it's Garrett who got me pregnant."

Jet shot her a confused look. "Why?"

"Garrett attended cowboy church the night after hooking up with me. He spent time talking to my dad, acting like this really good Christian, after totally ignoring me when we both arrived at the same time." She felt the same pain she felt then. "I don't think he knew I was Pastor Phillips's daughter." She hesitated. "I don't know if he even knew my name."

"Remind me why you liked him again?" Jet held up a

hand to keep her from answering. "That's a rhetorical question. I don't want to know anything else about him. He's just making me mad." He glanced at her. "Briar, if your mom was here, do you think you would have been able to confide in her?"

"I'd like to think so. Mom wasn't the least bit judgmental—but then, neither is Dad. I do wish Mom was here to talk to. I wish I'd talked to her when I had her, instead of giving her a hard time. I was too young to appreciate her, too angry."

"Why such a hothead, Phillips?"

"I wish I knew." She grimaced, aware she'd had a rebellious streak as long as she could remember.

When she was little, she didn't want to give her parents a hard time, but growing up Briar was often bored, and always restless. Even in kindergarten she didn't want to color within the lines. She hadn't cared if her handwriting was terrible. She didn't try to show her work in math, and even though it hurt her grade, she had the right answer, so why couldn't she do it in her head?

Why couldn't she just do life her way?

But doing life her way was proving incredibly problematic. Maybe it was time to color within the lines. Show her work. Follow the rules. "I need to tell my dad. I just don't know when."

Jet gave her a sympathetic glance. "You'll have a better idea of what to tell your dad once you talk to Garrett."

Her stomach fell, her insides churning. She dreaded facing Garrett. She dreaded the conversation, but soon it would be over, and she'd know what he wanted to do. "Yeah. I guess that's true."

※

BRIAR FOUND GARRETT over by his rig at the Fort Collins fairgrounds. It was a small rig, one that had seen better days. He was sitting outside the trailer, leaning back in a folding chair, hat pulled down low on his head shielding his eyes. He had a beer in his hand and a six-pack at his feet.

He pushed the brim of his hat up as she approached. "Briar Phillips," he said. "What brings you to Fort Collins?"

"So, you do know my name," she said, digging her hands into her vest pockets. "I wasn't so sure when you ignored me at my dad's church."

"If we're going to be honest, I didn't know your last name, or that you were related to Pastor Phillips, not until one of my friends told me later." He looked her up and down. "Come to get some more?"

"No. It wasn't that good the first time."

His smile faded. "Then what are you doing here, or are you just in town to ride another cowboy?"

She had to fight the urge to kick him. It would have felt good to kick him, but losing her temper wouldn't help any of them. "Not interested in hooking up or sex. Just thought I should let you know that—" She broke off, unsure now how to say it, unsure if she wanted him to know, but then she thought of the life growing inside of her and how she owed her daughter more. "I'm pregnant. We are pregnant," she clarified, pointing to him and then to herself. "The baby's due July second."

He smiled at her, a lazy amused smile, even as he drained his beer, dropping it at his side. The glass bottle clinked as it landed on the other empties. "We don't know that it's mine." Garrett kept smiling. "Fact is, I'm sure it's not mine. It could be anyone's—"

"No, it—" Briar wasn't about to tell him she was carrying a girl, not to a man who treated women so poorly. "It is." Her chin notched up, her expression grim. "It could only be yours. You were my first. You are still the only one I have slept with. There is no doubt in who created this baby."

"Not interested in being a daddy. Not interested in setting up house, getting married, don't want to be part of any of that."

"But you are going to be a daddy."

"No, I'm not. Not interested."

"So, why didn't you wear a condom?"

"Assumed you were on the pill." He smiled at her, an ugly smile. "Why didn't you ask me to wear a condom? Unless you wanted me to be the baby's daddy?"

"Why would I want to be a mom at twenty-two?"

"You can get rid of it."

"I'm in my third trimester."

"So?" He reached into his back pocket pulled out a battered leather wallet, opened it and drew out a number of bills. Rising, he thrust the crumpled bills into her hand. "This should take care of it," he said.

She looked down at her hand, and the four one-hundred-dollar bills. "What's this? To start a college fund?"

"There are always places who can handle these things—"

"*No.*" Briar's jaw firmed, and her lips compressed, holding back her disgust. "That was never an option."

"That's right. You're a sweet little church girl. Well, too bad, darlin'. This isn't my problem. I don't want it and I'm not going to pay child support and I'm not interested in having any relationship with it, so I've given you money to do the right thing. So, do the right thing and leave me alone."

"And what do I tell our baby? Your daddy didn't want you—"

He lunged toward her, hand raised. "Keep my name out of your mouth. Don't say anything about me. Don't send it my way. Got it?"

She wondered if he'd actually hit her if she continued to provoke him. And Briar was a hothead, but she wasn't interested in testing his self-control. "So that's it," she said glancing down at the four hundred dollars in her hand. "We're done?"

"So done. Now do us both a favor and get lost."

BRIAR'S LEGS SHOOK as she walked across the enormous

parking lot to where Jet was waiting for her. She climbed in and put on her seat belt without saying a word. She saw Jet glance at her, but he said nothing. And as they got back on the freeway, they were both silent. Briar couldn't bring herself to speak and Jet didn't ask questions.

But after a while, she couldn't keep all the emotion in. A tear fell, and she reached up to knock it away, and then another tear fell, and she tried to knock this one away, but she was fighting a losing battle.

Jet reached into his truck's center console, pulled out a little tissue packet and handed it to her.

"Thank you," she whispered, wiping her eyes and then blowing her nose.

"Want to talk about it?" he asked.

She shook her head. But then after a very long tortuous silence said, "He was such a jerk." Her voice cracked, broke. "He was awful."

"You caught him off guard. I'm sure when he gets used to the idea—"

"He gave me four hundred dollars toward an abortion. He told me to go fix it. I said I was in the third trimester and he didn't care. He doesn't want to see me again."

"I'm sorry."

"I'm not. Now I don't have to worry about him. I don't have to feel guilty for not doing the ethical thing. I told him. I told him the truth, and he said some pretty rude things, and now I can just focus on doing the best thing for me and the baby, whatever that is."

Chapter Nine

J ET WAS GLAD when Briar fell asleep, or pretended to sleep, hoping she had a release from the pain.

He was upset for her, livid that anyone would treat her so badly. He knew men were violent and cruel but poor Briar. She was still so innocent and still finding it hard to distinguish between the good guys and the bad guys.

Maybe there were men who genuinely didn't care about women, but Jet wasn't one of them, having felt a strong sense of responsibility for his mom even as a boy. During college he'd lived at home in Polson, and made the drive daily to Missoula, just so his mom wouldn't be alone. If she'd had a different personality, he would have been happy to stay on campus and be a student, but his mom had no family, and her only friends were women she knew at work, and they weren't the type to socialize outside of work.

His senior year at Missoula, he asked his mom if she thought she'd ever date again. She was still so pretty at thirty-eight, far too young to spend the rest of her life alone. She said maybe, one day, but she wasn't ready quite yet.

After graduating, Jet needed a career, and even though

aeronautics were out, he was intrigued by the idea of flying. He'd like to be a pilot and he approached a US Navy recruiter. There were plenty of prerequisites to even apply to the flight school, but he met them all. Jet didn't tell his mom he'd even applied to the Navy's fighter pilot program until after he'd been accepted. She was proud of him, but also emotional, knowing he'd be moving away. He reminded her that he'd be able to retire earlier than most, in his early forties, and he'd earn good money, too, enough to buy her that house she'd always dreamed of.

Jet had just been made a commissioned officer when he got word that his mom had been killed. Murdered.

At twenty-eight, he had every opportunity ahead of him and instead he imploded. He couldn't grieve, too angry to grieve, too angry she was gone, too angry with himself for not being there to protect her.

And when he heard that they couldn't press charges against the prime suspect, a man his mom had met on a dating site, he took matters into his own hands.

He tracked the man down and beat him within an inch of his life.

Jet was arrested, and he wouldn't have been able to make bail if it wasn't for a friend of his from the Navy flight school. He would have served a longer sentence if it wasn't for Pastor Patrick Phillips who traveled to Flathead County to see how he could help.

Thanks to his fellow Navy officers and Pastor Phillips's

support, Jet was saved from a long prison sentence, but his career was over. Worse, he wasn't someone that people wanted to hire. He wasn't someone people wanted to know.

He took a job in construction operating heavy machinery. The foreman was an ass and swore more than he spoke and then Jet got a job with a start-up in Denver—he was highly educated after all—but the wife of the owner freaked out when she heard Jet was a criminal who'd nearly beaten a man to death. Fired, Jet found a summer job in New Mexico on a dude ranch, and that seasonal work got him a full-time position at the Sundowner.

Jet didn't try to hide his past when he interviewed with Willis Love. He shared the same information with Cade Hunt and then the ranch owner, Dorothy Warner.

Cade told him to come to Wyoming and they'd try him out. That was fourteen months ago, and he liked the Sundowner, but he also knew life was full of change, and nothing lasted forever.

An hour later Briar stretched and opened her eyes. Blinking, she looked around. "Where are we?"

"A half hour from Capser."

She sat up straight. "Already?"

"You've been asleep for a bit." He smiled at her. "But that's good. You needed it."

She combed her fingers through her long dark hair, trying to tidy it. "We're going to be back on the ranch in time for dinner."

Jet nodded. "Speaking of food, are you hungry? I'm starving."

"I could use food," she agreed.

"There's a good little café in Casper. Homestyle cooking at its best."

"That works for me."

Twenty minutes later, Jet pulled into the restaurant's parking lot. As it was two o'clock on Sunday, there were parking spaces available and inside a half dozen open tables. The waitress told them to sit where they liked and followed with a pair of menus. Jet glanced at Briar to see where she wanted to sit.

Briar shook her head. "I don't care."

They both ordered the same thing—the fried chicken, mashed potatoes and gravy, and the café's famous buttermilk biscuits. They didn't say much while waiting for their food and when it arrived, they focused on their plates. But when finished, Jet saw Briar's eyes fill with tears and her pain made him hurt.

"I'm sorry, Briar. Sorry that Garrett Jones is such a piece of work."

She used her paper napkin to dab her eyes. "How did you find out his last name?"

"Looked him up on the Fort Collins rodeo website. They list the competitors. He's a steer wrestler."

She looked away, lips pinched, expression heartsick.

"You need to stop hating on yourself," he said. "You're

just a person. Everyone makes mistakes."

"I just feel like I've made way too many."

"You're twenty-two. Give yourself a break."

"I'm old enough to know better. I can't blame anyone else but me."

"You're still young—and I'm not trying to be condescending. Maturity doesn't come all at once. I'm thirty-two and I still don't feel mature."

"Wow," she said, trying to make a joke "I had no idea you were so old." And then she smiled, her first smile of the day. "Besides beating a guy up, what mistakes have you made?"

"I drank a lot the year after I was kicked out of the Navy. That was a mistake. I don't drink now."

"Never?"

"Never."

"You don't miss it?"

He felt as if she'd punched him, and it was the strangest reaction to such a simple question. "I don't miss liquor," he said quietly. "But I do miss Mom."

She reached out and touched the back of his hand. "I am sorry. Really sorry."

He turned her hand over so her palm was against his. "After seeing Garrett, have you thought any more on what you want to do?"

"I'm keeping my baby," she said firmly. "I can't give her away. She's mine." She slipped her hand from his, slid out from the booth and left the table to use the ladies' room.

IN THE BATHROOM, Briar put cold water on her eyes and then looking at herself in the mirror gave herself a stern mental lecture. *No more tears, Briar. No more being weak. You have to be strong from now on.*

By the time she returned to the table their dishes were cleared away and Jet had a fresh cup of coffee, and she had a cup of herbal tea waiting for her.

"I didn't know if you'd want dessert," he said gruffly.

She shook her head. "Not today but the tea is great. Thank you."

"It's mint, I think."

She smiled faintly. "I do like mint." But it was very hot tea, and she couldn't drink it immediately. "I hope we'll be home before Cade. It might be awkward to roll up at the same time as him."

"He's going to know we were together. Your truck is there. We both were absent all day."

"I really don't want to deal with him today. I don't have the energy. We will just get into it, and I'll say something I'll regret later."

"What will he object most to? That you're pregnant, or you're single?"

"That I'm single and pregnant, without any real income of my own."

"Is he afraid he's going to have to be responsible for you?"

She sighed. "I don't know. Maybe? But he's wrong. I wouldn't ever let that happen. I don't want anyone to be responsible for me. I'm responsible for myself."

"You're going to need support from somewhere. You can't do it all on your own."

"I'm not going to ask Miss Warner for help, either."

"Let me help you," he said.

She frowned at him as she lifted her steaming cup. "I'm not going to take your money, Jet."

"If we married it wouldn't be my money. It'd be our money."

Briar set the cup down swiftly, tea sloshing over the rim. "I think I misunderstood what you just said."

"You didn't."

Her nerves tightened and tingled. She couldn't believe what she'd heard. "You're suggesting marriage."

"Yes."

"Why?"

"Because it's something I could do that would make your life easier, and if I can do that, I want to."

"Why?" she repeated stubbornly.

"Your dad helped me when I needed someone, and if I can help you, then I've finally done something good."

She shook her head, confused and offended. "So, this is about my dad?"

"No. It's about you, Briar. It's about giving you a hand hoping you'll take it, hoping you'll feel supported so you can keep your baby and be the mom you want to be."

"Jet, you're not just offering a hand, you are offering marriage. That's pretty crazy. Who does that?"

"Fortunately, it's easy to get married in Las Vegas. It's fast. It could be done in a day. Well, two days if you include travel time."

"Just fly to Las Vegas and get married. It's as easy as that," Briar said, struggling to smile.

In some ways his suggestion was a dream. She was infatuated with Jet. She loved spending time with him, but he didn't love her, and she couldn't imagine how he'd feel in a year's time, never mind five or ten years.

"You're still not really showing but you won't be able to hide it forever. If we got married now, you won't have to put up with any speculation from anyone—"

"Oh, there will be speculation," she corrected.

"But you'll have a ring on your finger, and it's no one's business but ours."

"So says the man without a family."

Her sarcasm was sharp, but Jet merely lifted a brow. "It's not as if I wanted to be alone in the world," he said mildly.

Briar winced. "I'm sorry. That was uncalled for. I shouldn't take my frustration out on you. You've done so much for me, and I'm grateful. I might not sound grateful, but I am."

"I'm not looking for gratitude," he said gruffly.

"Then what are you doing this for?"

He hesitated. "I don't know. Honor, maybe?"

"You weren't the one that got me pregnant."

He said nothing to this, and she squirmed inwardly, overwhelmed by virtually everything. She didn't know what she'd expected from Garrett today but certainly not derision followed by a wad of cash to pay for an abortion. And while she didn't expect Garrett to propose, she'd thought he might care a little bit about the life he helped make. Jet had been a hero driving her down to Fort Collins, but she did not expect him to take her on along with the baby. "We have very little in common. Until fairly recently, we could barely tolerate the other. In fact, the only reason you're being nice to me now is because you know I'm in trouble."

The corner of his mouth lifted. "I wouldn't say you're in trouble. I would say you're in a situation."

"Semantics aside," she said. "We barely know each other."

"We know each other better than you knew Garrett."

She exhaled hard. "True."

Jet's set jaw eased. "We can't change the past. One can only go forward, and hopefully, make better choices."

She was finally able to sip from her tea. It was strong and hot, and she took another small sip.

Would marrying Jet be considered making a good choice? Somehow, she doubted her dad would see it that way—unless he thought the baby was Jet's, and then he might feel differently. But how was it fair to put Jet in that position? She'd essentially be throwing him under the bus, and it wasn't right. Cade would lose his mind. Cade would—

She shook her head. "Cade would fire you," she said. "I can't let you be the fall guy. You deserve better than that."

"I'm not worried about me. I'm worried about you, and your little girl, who will be here before you know it. And then what? How will you support yourself? How will you juggle it all?"

"I don't know, but marriage is serious. It's a lifelong commitment. It's not something one just rushes into."

"Like unprotected sex with a stranger?"

Briar cringed. "Stop it." She hated that he was right. "I am trying to make good choices, Jet. I'm trying to be a responsible mom."

"How is trying to do it all on your own a better choice? Who is going to support you? Who will take care of the baby while you work? Obviously if you return home, your dad will help you—"

"I'm not doing that."

"Then Cade?"

"*No.*" She shuddered. "I love him, but no way. He's already overbearing."

"So, what's your plan?"

"I don't know, but you can't be my plan. It doesn't make

sense. It's completely illogical."

"Like being a single mom is logical?"

"If that's my situation."

"So where do you live? How do you do this?"

Furious, Briar leaned across the table. "I have no idea why *you* would do this. Are you desperate to be a dad? Are you longing to be a family man? Is there something you want to tell me, cowboy?"

He studied her for a long moment before his dense lashes dropped, concealing his expression. "I'm concerned for you. I'm concerned for your child. No child wants to grow up without a dad. Single moms have it hard. Single moms don't get enough respect."

"You have a lot of experience with single moms then?"

Jet reached into his pocket and drew out a couple of twenty-dollar bills. "My mom was one. She got pregnant at sixteen, had me just before she turned seventeen. We were two kids raising each other. I got lucky that she didn't introduce a whole bunch of losers to me, that she waited to date until I was out of the house, but it wasn't easy on her. She was treated differently than the other moms at my school, and I was treated differently than the other kids. It's not what I would wish for you or your baby." He rose from the booth, reached for his coat. "Ready to go?"

She blinked, caught off guard, and got to her feet more slowly, murmuring thanks as Jet helped her with her coat. "Why would you want to raise someone else's kid?" she asked softly as she zipped her coat closed.

"Because if I can help, then I should." He didn't wait for an answer. He started walking for the door.

Briar watched him for a moment, stunned, and then she grabbed her purse and quickly followed. "Jet—"

"Let's not talk right now," he said, opening the passenger door for her. "Let's leave it alone for now. We don't need to make a decision today. We don't even have to think about it today. Let's just get you back to the ranch, okay?"

But inside the truck Briar couldn't help thinking about his suggestion. She couldn't help thinking about how protective he was toward his mom. How he felt compelled to help her. She also wondered about the favor her father had done for him.

After a half hour she broke the silence. "Jet?"

"Hmm?"

She noticed he didn't even take his eyes off the road. "Can I ask you one question?"

"Sure."

"What did my dad do for you?"

"Through his ministry, he knew my relatives—not that I've ever met them—and he'd met my mom once, but he didn't know me. But after I was arrested, he came to see me, and he told me that I could count on him, that I could trust him, and that if there was anything he could do for me he would.

"I was shocked," Jet added after a moment, "reminding

him he didn't know me, and I didn't know why I deserved his help. And do you know what your father said?"

Briar shook her head.

"He said, 'I never had a son, but I would hope that if I did and he was in trouble, someone would be there for him. I'd hope someone would reach out and offer support and show him love. Everybody makes mistakes, and I think everyone deserves a second chance.'" Jet exhaled slowly. "I had friends who vouched for me, but if it hadn't been for your father, I could have, would have, served years. Instead, after a brief time in jail, I ended up going into a work program and doing community service, and then I found a job."

"Why didn't you tell me this before?"

Jet shrugged. "It was between us, but that's why I'm grateful to your dad, and that's why if I can do him a good turn I would want to."

"Marrying his wayward daughter is more than a good turn."

"I don't know that he'd see it that way."

"No?"

"No. Your dad is a compassionate man, but I can't imagine he'd want me as a son-in-law."

"You didn't kill anyone, Jet."

"Don't defend me, Briar."

"I'm just saying. You didn't kill him. You taught him a lesson. And sometimes that's a good thing."

"Your dad wouldn't agree. Remember 'Vengence is mine, said the Lord.'"

"Maybe I'm not a proper Christian, but I can't condemn you. If I were you, I would have done the same thing."

THEY ARRIVED BACK at the Sundowner Ranch a few minutes before five, giving Briar time to scoot upstairs to her room and take a shower and clean up for dinner. But in the shower, she played back the day, and Garrett's ugly words came back to her, and then Jet's proposal, and it tangled her up. Could two men be any more different?

As Briar toweled off and then began dressing, she wished she could have dinner in her room, but Miss Warner's house wasn't a hotel, and you didn't miss dinner unless you were ill.

With her hair in a long sleek braid and her denim blouse layered over a T-shirt, she hoped she looked nice enough for Sunday dinner. She also hoped if Cade was there, he wouldn't make a comment about her weight. But at some point, everyone would notice. She wasn't going to be able to hide her pregnancy much longer.

Was getting married a solution? Jet seemed to think it was. But in her mind, she feared she'd be jumping from the fire into the frying pan.

But at least it would be Jet's frying pan.

Briar paused on the staircase, hearing voices in the dining

room. There were two men speaking. Was it Cade and Jet? If so, why had Miss Warner invited Jet tonight? She knew Cade didn't like Jet around his sister.

But entering the dining room, she saw it wasn't just Cade and MerriBee with Grace. It was a man she didn't recognize talking to Jet and Miss Warner.

Briar went over to her sister-in-law and kissed her cheek and smiled at Grace who drew back to hide her face in her mother's shoulder.

Briar tickled the back of Grace's neck. "I still see you," Briar teased.

Grace turned her head and peeked at Briar giving her a shy smile.

"Have a good day?" Cade asked Briar.

Briar nodded. "I did, thank you. How did your meeting go in Yellowstone?"

"Well," Cade answered. "I liked Aaron Welks so well that I invited him home for dinner so Dot could meet him and decide if she was interested in his film project."

Briar glanced toward Miss Warner, Jet, and the filmmaker. They were all engrossed in conversation, but Jet's head lifted, and his piercing blue gaze briefly met hers and held.

Heat rushed through her, and she felt a frisson of pleasure. He was so handsome. And yes, she had a crush on him, maybe more than a crush, but was she ready to marry? Not just him, but anyone? She didn't feel ready for marriage. But then, she hadn't been ready for becoming a mother, but it was happening with or without her consent.

Dinner was a blur of conversation and Briar was thankful she wasn't needed to say anything as she couldn't focus on anything but the baby who'd be making an appearance in three months. She did need a plan. She needed a home. Somewhere safe.

She looked across the table at Jet. He was playing peekaboo with Grace, the tray of her wooden high chair higher than the table. Briar had polished the antique high chair several times since she'd arrived at the Sundowner, Emma having shared that it had been Miss Warner's when she was a baby and Willis had pulled it out of the attic for little Grace.

Grace was laughing at Jet's antics, giggling when he hid behind the napkin and Briar couldn't tear her gaze away. Jet was so sweet and patient with Grace. Briar suspected he'd be a good father, but what did she know?

What did she know about anything?

Aware that eyes were on her, she looked around and discovered Cade watching her. His expression puzzled her. He didn't look angry as much as sad. She didn't know why he'd look at her with sadness. Briar would have to talk to him. She didn't like this awful distance and tension between them.

It bothered her that she couldn't get it right with him. He didn't seem to understand how important he was to her, and how much she valued his good opinion.

Dinner ended when Miss Warner finally rose and MerriBee carried Grace to Dot so Grace could kiss her good night. Jet walked the filmmaker out to his car. Cade escorted Dot into her family room. Briar cleared the table and filled the sink, prepared to tackle dishes before she joined Miss Warner for TV. But Cade joined her almost immediately in the kitchen.

"I'll help you," he offered, rolling up his sleeves.

"Don't you want to keep Dot company?" Briar asked.

"She was the one that suggested I help with the dishes. She didn't want you to be left all alone in here."

"I love her," Briar said simply, sincerely.

Miss Warner had become the aunt/grandmother mentor she'd never had and didn't realize until now how much she needed her.

"Did you know our grandmother, Suzy's mother?" Briar asked Cade as she quickly scraped the plates into the compost pail.

"I saw her a few times when I was little," he said, filling the sink with hot water and adding a generous squeeze of dish soap. "But as I got older, Mom and I stopped visiting. I don't think Jimmy liked Mom going there. I don't know why, and I don't think I ever asked Mom, either. It just seemed better not to ask questions."

"You mean, like I do?" Briar said, gently teasing her brother.

"Of course you're curious. I would be if I were you."

She took a clean towel from the drawer. "I know you've

told me that I look like Mom, but what was she *like*? Outgoing? Quiet? Serious? Funny? Did she talk a lot? Did she laugh or tell jokes?"

"She was mostly quiet, at least by the time I was old enough to know her. I think she was different when she was younger. I think—I know—she had a wild streak and made some bad choices. Some of those choices really hurt her."

Briar began drying the first plate. "Getting pregnant with me?"

"Mom's trouble started long before you. Her problems started with the way she was raised, and how her dad was really cold and angry. I don't think he treated Mom or Grandmother very nicely. He had a temper and took his anger out on them. It was especially bad after he'd been drinking."

"Poor Mom. My parents, Joany and Patrick, were nothing like that. They were wonderful. They loved me so much. So much. I wasn't always the easiest daughter."

"Our mom, Suzy, she loved you, too. She wanted you, but she couldn't bring you home to Jimmy. Jimmy wasn't a good guy. It's ironic how she left home early to get away from her dad, and then later married someone even worse than her dad."

"Do you ever wonder about your biological dad?" Cade asked, handing her another plate.

"Not really. I love my dad so much. I know I've given him grief, but he's the best dad and I never cared about meeting whoever sired me." She set the dry plate down and reached for another. "Are you glad you found the Wyatts?"

"I'm glad I found them while Melvin was still alive. He's a really solid man. Has tremendous integrity. He's kept that family together. I admire him a lot."

"I have this story in my head," Briar said, drying and talking, "that Suzy and my biological father met at Grey's Saloon in Marietta, had some drinks and then they went to his room at the Graff and fell into bed together. They had this great night and then it was over, and he was gone leaving Suzy pregnant." *Much like me.*

"It sounds quite plausible," Cade admitted. "And in many ways, I can't blame Mom for seeking out the company of strangers. Jimmy was hard on her. He used her like a punching bag, until I was old enough to get in between."

"Did he hit you then?"

Cade shrugged. "It was better than him hitting Mom."

Briar suddenly wrapped her arms around Cade and hugged him fiercely. "I love you, Cade. And maybe I'm not the sister you expected, it's like that insurance commercial, I'm the sister you've got."

He kissed the top of her head. "Don't ever feel that way," he protested, voice husky. "You're exactly as you should be. And you remind me so much of Mom that it sometimes takes my breath away."

"Because I'm trouble?"

"No. You're so beautiful. You remind me of Mom before life sucked the joy out of her. I hope you never lose you, Briar. You're perfect the way you are."

Chapter Ten

Life on the ranch was always busy, but the next day after having finished her work until she needed to return to help with dinner, Briar headed to the barn. She spent a long time grooming Judas but he kept nudging her in the shoulder. He wanted out. He wanted to move. She did, too. Surely it wouldn't hurt her or the baby if they kept to a walk. She'd grown up riding, and from what she'd read, the greatest danger from riding while pregnant was falling, and she wasn't going to fall. Briar knew what her body could and couldn't do.

It didn't take long for her to get Judas saddled and they were off. For the first half hour she didn't think, too relieved to be outside, breathing in the crisp mountain air, savoring the sun on her face. She was a Montanan, through and through, and yet she felt at home here in Wyoming. Maybe it was the mountains, the big sky, the larger-than-life personalities. Or maybe it was the same rugged lifestyle. She wasn't a city girl, would never be a city girl, and her happiest times were like this—outside, on her horse, being herself. Feeling free.

She'd just turned Judas back toward the ranch when Jet appeared in the distance. He was riding fast, and as he approached, he eased his horse from a gallop to a canter and then finally a trot.

Briar's heart beat faster and she sat up in her saddle, enthralled by the way he rode. He was handsome and he gave her butterflies. He had an inexplicable way of making her feel and feel better. Stronger and safer. She was incredibly attracted to him, but was that a good enough reason to marry him?

Her brain said she shouldn't consider the option, that it wasn't a realistic solution, but her heart wasn't so sure. Maybe they could be happy together. Maybe he could learn to love her. She knew he didn't love her now. It was responding to duty. He felt an obligation to offer for her. It was probably the same reason he'd joined the Navy. It was a job he could do, so he did it.

Jet drew up next to her. "I got worried about you," he said. "You've been gone a long time."

She arched a brow. "Keeping track of me?"

"Always."

She reined in Judas, bringing him to a stop. "Why?"

"When Cade was gone, it was my job."

"But he's back now," she said.

"Now it's a choice." His lips curved faintly. "Besides, I'd rather think about you than Ace or Rolly or Brent."

"Thank you, I think." She eased the rein and encouraged

Judas to begin walking again. "You and Cade were in a meeting with Miss Warner all lunch. Everything okay?"

"Miss Warner has found some property she's interested in purchasing. There are two different farms available right now, one north of Story, on the way to Sheridan, and the other just outside Buffalo. This morning Cade and I viewed both. She wanted Cade's opinion."

"But she asked you a lot of questions, too," Briar said, looking at him from beneath the brim of her hat. "She actually asked you more questions than Cade."

"Only because I've become her hay expert."

Briar thought he sounded amused. "I suppose it's a little bit different from wanting to be an astronaut."

He shrugged. "It is, but agriculture is a science, and I enjoy learning new things, so it's not a problem." For a moment they rode side by side, and it was a comfortable silence. Although to be fair it wasn't silent. The breeze played across the hills, rustling the grass. Birds chirped and twittered. Cows mooed in the distance.

"Have you thought any more about my suggestion, or about what you want to do?" Jet asked as the house, barn, and outbuildings came into view.

She knew there were so many reasons why she shouldn't even consider Jet's proposal. Chiefly, Cade, her dad, maybe even Miss Warner.

But she had been considering the suggestion and even though she hadn't planned on getting married so young, she thought marriage to Jet wouldn't be terrible. She was drawn to him, and felt happier when with him, but it wasn't fair to him. He hadn't put her in this situation, and it wasn't right to have him be the one to bail her out.

So, no, she shouldn't even consider it.

But she was.

Maybe it was because she had a history of being impulsive. Or maybe it was because she was a hothead who had stupidly jumped into bed with Garrett, imagining some wonderful experience—now *that* still blew her mind. So maybe that was why she could *almost* imagine herself doing something just as stupid with Jet.

If she took away the emotions, if she took away all the objections, marrying Jet would solve some very real problems.

Her baby would have a father.

She would have a husband, important when living in a conservative community, helping shield her daughter from criticism and speculation.

If something happened to her, her daughter would still be protected and have a family.

That last one was perhaps the most important. Briar wasn't fatalistic, but things happened and even she, with her meager faith, felt the hand of providence in Jet's proposal. Her dad would be a good grandfather, but he wasn't meant to raise another child, not at his age, not by himself, which was how it would be if something happened to her.

No, her baby needed a young, healthy, responsible father, one that would take an active role in raising her, one that would be present, one that would be patient, too.

Would Jet be that father? She didn't know him as well as she'd like, but her gut said he was honest. Honorable. A man with integrity. He'd certainly been straight forward, but also kind, with her. "I have been thinking a lot about our conversation from the drive back from Fort Collins."

Jet looked at her and waited.

"I think about it a lot at night. It's in my mind as I'm working," she added. "Sometimes I feel like it's all I think about."

"It's a big decision," he said.

"Very big," she agreed, glancing at him, and just that one glance, her pulse quickened and her stomach did a dizzying flip. He was tall and tough, physical and powerful, and she had a definite soft spot for his gorgeous face, and those blue eyes of his, which seemed to see far too much of everything.

Suddenly the nervous knots in her middle were so intense she thought she might throw up. "I think I want to walk," she said, stopping Judas. "But you can go ahead—"

"No. I'm happy to walk, too." He swung his leg over his horse's back and stepped down.

She tried not to focus on his butt and legs, but they were strong, and lean, and she found herself wondering what it might have been like, if her first time had been with him instead of Garrett.

Judas did a side step as she dismounted, and Jet reached out, steadied Judas, which she appreciated as her legs felt like jelly. Her body felt odd. Not sick, just different. Everything lately felt different. She was beginning to feel awkward, her center of gravity changing, her muscles and tendons achy.

Right as she stepped onto the ground, the baby kicked, hard and Briar gasped and put a hand to her middle. "Wow."

"What's wrong?" Jet asked, stepping toward her, taking Judas's bridle.

"She kicked me. Hard." Briar looked up at him, and then laughed. "She's not playing around." And then her smile faded, and Briar felt exposed. Vulnerable. "You know the expression, beggars can't be choosers?" she said, looking up at Jet.

"I do."

"I'm a beggar, but I'm going to be choosy."

"As you should. You have options. You can afford to be choosy."

She didn't know what it was about the way he talked to her, but it resonated with her, connecting within her to a place no one else could touch. He made her feel rational. Reasonable. Strong. They'd known each other just a few weeks but in that time he'd become someone she trusted, someone she considered a friend.

"So, here's the thing. I need to know, straight up, the truth." Briar faced him, hands digging into her back pockets, shoulders squared. "Would you be a good dad? Would you be patient? Would you be kind?" Her voice quavered, and she lifted her chin, fighting the emotion building inside of her. "I don't expect anyone to be perfect, and we all know I have a temper, and it's natural to become short-tempered, especially when tired or stressed, but I feel strongly that there are ways to punish other than hitting. For example, spanking ... my parents didn't spank me. I know a lot of people feel like a well-placed swat on the behind isn't a bad thing, but I'm uncomfortable getting overly physical. Corporal punishment bothers me. Now there are probably plenty of people who would say, I could have benefitted from a proper spanking or two, but my parents didn't believe in that, and now that I'm about to become a mom, I don't believe in it, too." She looked up into Jet's face, trying to read his expression. "What do you think?"

"My mother never once hit me. I can't imagine hitting a child—or a teenager. Or anyone in my family. Family is family. To be protected forever."

"Good."

"What else?" he asked.

"I would hope—no, expect for you to be involved. It's not enough to put your name on the birth certificate. You wouldn't be a father in name only. If we marry, I'm marrying you, you'd be the father. You'd be Dad." Her eyes searched his. "You'd be one of the two most important people in her life, and being a dad is really important. Being there through hard times is important." Her voice cracked. "I know you didn't have a dad, not like the one I had, but I'd hope you would show up for all the school things, and the sports, and teach her about important life things. I just would hope you'd love her."

"Of course," he said quietly.

Her eyes welled with tears. She struggled to continue and glanced away, fighting for composure. "It's a lot to ask, but it's the only way this could work, and if it's too big of an ask, we won't do this. I can't do this. Because if you are miserable, we will all be miserable, and that's not fair to anyone."

"And what is this big ask?"

"That we be united, as much as possible, for her sake, and any other children we might have." Briar blushed, her cheeks burning. She forced herself to meet Jet's piercing gaze. "I'm not going into this expecting it to be a bed of roses, but at the same time, I'm not going into this wanting to be single later. I don't want us to marry if we're not going to take the vows seriously. I don't want to get married to end up divorced. My parents had a very good marriage, a loving relationship, and while I don't expect you to give me chocolates and flowers, I'd like us to be friends, and maybe eventually, there will be love."

"Are you afraid I'll make you miserable?" he asked, a wry note in his deep voice.

His deep husky voice made her grow warmer and she tried to check her pulse, her heart racing far too fast. It wasn't a hardship being around Jet. He was attractive, really attractive, and rugged and masculine and all the things she found appealing. He also had a conscience, a strong moral compass, and if something didn't sit well with him, he said so. She appreciated that, far better to spend a life with someone who was honest. Straightforward. She hated trying to read between the lines.

And then there was this unsettling effect he had on her, the butterflies he gave her, the breathless sensation she got when their eyes met. She didn't know what this was—attraction? Infatuation?—but it was something and it filled her, buoyed her, gave her hope. "No," she whispered, mouth drying, heart thudding. "I like you."

"Good. I like you, too." And then he closed the rest of the distance between them, tipped her head up and kissed her, a slow, head-spinning kiss that was as much an exploration of her mouth as it was of her skin, her heart, her soul.

Kissing him, so many confusing pieces settled into place.

She was infatuated. More than infatuated. She'd been falling for him ever since she met him and she'd wanted this kiss, wanted his touch, and she wanted to accept his proposal but at the same time, it wasn't fair to him. He shouldn't have to sacrifice his future for her. He shouldn't have to be the strong moral compass in her chaotic world.

But as he deepened the kiss, drawing her even closer, it became impossible to think when she craved him and his touch. Her knees wobbled and her legs were weak. She trembled against him, and Jet's arm came around her waist, holding her securely, making her feel things she didn't think she'd ever feel.

The intensity of her emotions caught her off guard. She wanted him—his company, his conversation, his comfort, his passion, his laughter, his confidence.

His tongue teased hers, stroking, flicking setting nerves alight. She shivered at the pleasure, feeling her bones melt, her muscles heat, her veins filled with something hot and sweet. Jet cupped her cheek, his thumb stroking lightly across her hot cheekbone and jaw, exploring her face and then just below her mouth. He filled her senses, overwhelming completely and she shivered again, a shudder of desire, need and want making her burn.

Finally, his head lifted, and he looked down into her face, his eyes dark, his features hard, expression intent. "There's no reason we can't be happy. I will be a good husband. There won't be anyone else. I will always be faithful to you. I will always be honest with you. I promise to put you and our children first."

She flushed, and ached, her lower belly tightening, hungry for pressure, pleasure, release. But it wasn't just her body tingling and aching. Her heart ached, too. Jet was saying the right words, but it worried her that she was already falling for him so hard.

Would she be okay living with a man who respected her, and was kind to her, but didn't love her? Could she live without his love? Or could she trust that over time love would come?

"We will have children of our own, too, won't we?" she asked unsteadily.

"I would hope so." He traced her mouth, and her lips quivered and parted. He stroked her full lip with the pad of his thumb, sending sharp darts of sensation everywhere.

"Yes," she said, squeezing her thighs together, and holding her breath, containing the yearning. She wanted love, wanted to be loved, but the baby came first. "I accept your offer. If you're still willing."

His gaze held hers. "I am."

A tremor raced through her. Her skin tingled as she went hot, then cold. "Good." Briar swallowed hard. "When?"

He didn't even hesitate. "Tomorrow."

Her insides did a wild tumble. She blinked up at Jet. Married to this darkly handsome cowboy tomorrow? She couldn't even wrap her head around it. "What do we tell everyone?"

"Don't worry about that. Just be ready to go early in the morning."

"How early?"

"I'll text you later today. I've some arrangements to make. I'll also be sending you a link. It's the application for our marriage license. If we do it tonight, it'll be ready for us to pick up in the morning."

"That's all we need to do?"

"We need it for the ceremony. But the service itself is short."

"How do you know all of this? Have you been married in Las Vegas before?"

His jaw eased. He almost smiled. "No. But I know a few people who have. It's ridiculously easy. No blood test required. We'll be married by tomorrow night."

※

AS BRIAR RETURNED to her room Jet's words kept echoing in her head. *We'll be married by tomorrow night.*

She stripped off her riding clothes and took a shower, thinking about all the things that had to happen between now and then. Briar knew it was a long drive from Bozeman to Las Vegas, and it would be even longer from Wyoming. After her shower, still wrapped in a bath towel, she checked the flights from Billings, as that would be the closest airport from the Sundowner.

There were no direct flights, mostly flights with two stops. There was a one-stop flight but it left just after five a.m., which meant they'd have to leave the ranch by two in the morning if they wanted to make it, and that was still cutting it close. So, flights with two stops it would be, making it at least a nine-to-thirteen-hour flight, and that was without the drive to the airport. Would driving to Vegas be any better?

A quickie wedding would mean two days from the ranch.

She'd have to say something to Cade and Miss Warner, but what?

After dressing, Briar considered her wardrobe and what she'd need to pack. It was a Las Vegas wedding, so she didn't need much. Her jeans, a blouse or two, pajamas and, of course, her favorite cowboy boots. She'd add her toiletries just before she went to bed.

Briar was just about to head down to the kitchen when she got a text from Jet. *I've just sent you the link for the license. Also, Cade and I won't be back for dinner. I might not be back until late, but don't worry, we'll still head out early in the morning. I'll pick you up outside the house at four.*

She knew why he'd decided it would be four. No one else should be up then. But why were Cade and Jet not returning for dinner? Where had they gone?

Miss Warner filled Briar in over dinner, breaking the news that she'd purchased Gilstrap Ranch in Buffalo and Cade was handling the paperwork with the Realtor while Jet was inspecting the ranch, assessing where they'd need to make the improvements if they hoped to get new seed in the group.

Briar had heard so much over the past few weeks about hay production in Johnson County that she understood most of what Miss Warner was telling her. The big producers in Johnson, like the Gilstrap Ranch, put up more than 94,000 tons of hay. In terms of revenue, it was the county's second-largest agricultural product behind beef. Miss Warner had been itching to increase the Sundowner's hay yield as it would help out the Sundowner, but it'd also become another revenue stream.

Normally Briar would be happy to linger over dinner and watch TV and have dessert, but tonight she had a hard time sitting still. Pleading a headache, she made an escape to her room where she tackled the form required. It was very basic stuff. Her parents' names, where she was born, stuff like that. By the time she was finished she felt numb.

Was this really going to happen?

Knowing that a four a.m. pickup meant waking even earlier, Briar packed the rest of her things and climbed into bed. Once in bed, she sent Jet a text. *I finished my part of the application.*

He replied almost right away. *I'll handle the payment when I get back.*

Where are you? she asked.

Heading up the ranch road now. Should be home in ten.

Briar swallowed her nervousness. *Are you still picking me up at four?*

Yes.

She looked at the little dancing dots indicating he was typing something else.

Having second thoughts? he asked.

Her fingers trembled as she texted back. *No. Just want to make sure you're not.*

I'm not.

She stared at his answer for a long moment, and then slowly exhaled. *See you at four*, she texted.

See you soon, he answered. *Good night.*

Chapter Eleven

J ET WAS OUTSIDE as he'd said he would be, sitting in his truck in the dark, lights off, engine off when she stepped out of the house at four.

Once they'd left the ranch and were on the road that led to the highway, Jet filled her in on their plan. A friend of his, a fellow Navy pilot, Vander Campbell, would be meeting them at the airstrip in Sheridan and flying them in his private plane to the executive terminal in Las Vegas.

It would only take a couple of hours that way, Jet explained, instead of half a day.

Jet was clearly pleased with the arrangement, but Briar had only flown once before, and it had been on a big plane years ago and she had been a little nervous even then. "Are you sure we shouldn't just drive?" she asked faintly. "I mean, if we drove straight to Vegas now, we'd get there by tonight, and the wedding chapels are open at night, aren't they?"

"It's a really long drive," he answered. "It's normally fourteen and a half hours from here, but Willis was telling me about a big construction project in Utah that has the freeway narrowing to one lane just outside Salt Lake. It's causing really bad backups, adding a couple hours or more. I can't see spending sixteen or seventeen hours in the car when we could be there it two or three."

He made a good point, but he also didn't realize not everyone was used to zipping around in the sky. "But isn't driving safer?"

"No." He took off his hat and ran his hand through his hair, leaving his hat upside down on the console between them. "Not for those of us who know what we're doing, and Vander is one of the best. Nothing bad is going to happen, I promise."

"I heard Miss Warner and Emma talking about a new weather front moving in ... could be quite a storm. Have you heard that, too?"

"Cade and I were discussing it last night. There could be snow, but my plan is that we'll be back before then. I'd like to fly in and out today, which should get us home in plenty of time." He looked at her, expression somber. "We won't take any risks, though. I'd never put you in harm's way. You know that, don't you?"

She nodded. It was one of the reasons she'd decided to marry him. In a world where things could get topsy-turvy, she knew he'd always be a straight arrow pointing to truth. "I do trust you," she said. "It's just that I've only flown once. It was a regular plane, a United jet. I know you said your friend was in the Navy with you, but little planes seem so dangerous. Is your friend still in the Navy, or has he left? Does he still fly a lot? How experienced is he compared to you?"

"More." Jet smiled at her. "He's still a Navy fighter pilot. He's one of the best the Navy has. Vander's only around because he's on leave for a couple weeks, visiting family in Montana. His uncle has a place in Paradise Valley. Cold Canyon Ranch. Do you know it?"

"No, but unless they breed horses, I don't tend to pay much attention to all the different folks out there."

"If after meeting Vander you're still not comfortable, we'll just get back in the truck and drive to Las Vegas. I'm not going to make you do anything you don't want to do. Just let me know what you think when we get to Sheridan and see the plane and meet my friend."

When they reached Sheridan an hour later, Jet introduced her to Vander—or Van, as Jet called him—and Briar was immediately put at ease, along with being a little starstruck. Van looked like he'd just walked off a movie set, with his tall, lean, athletic frame. He was tan and attractive with cropped hair, chiseled features, and a strong, square jaw. He had to be in his thirties, and when he shook her hand, Vander looked into her eyes and smiled. "I understand you're my VIP today," he said.

"I don't know about being a VIP," she said, a little dazzled because his crooked smile did nothing to diminish his air of authority. The man was confident, and completely in control.

Briar glanced at Jet and wondered if this was how Jet was

before—she broke off, and swallowed, surprised by the sharpness of the pang in her chest.

She wasn't the only one who'd been through a lot. Jet had suffered horrific losses and yet he was still here. Tough, strong, a leader. She reached for Jet's hand and held it tightly. "I'm good to do this," she said.

Jet's lips barely curved but she saw the flare of heat in his eyes. "Good," he said quietly. "But, Briar, there is no pressure—"

"I'm fine," she said, taking her hand back, self-conscious that she'd reached for him. It had been such an instinctive gesture. "Honestly."

"Then let's do this," Vander said. He walked them to his plane and Jet helped get her settled in the backseat.

"Do you want me sitting back here with you," Jet asked her. "Or would you mind if I'm up front with Van? I haven't been flying in years and I'd love to be in the cockpit but not if it'll make you anxious."

"I won't be anxious. In fact, I think I'll feel even better if you were up there," she whispered. "Besides, it'd be fun to see you in action."

Jet's gaze met hers and held. The spark was back, that bright heat and light that sent a thrill through her.

"Vander's in charge," Jet said, even as he double-checked her seat belt. "I'm just his copilot today."

I love you. She stopped herself before the words were spoken. Instead, she caught him by the coat, and held it for a split second. "Thank you."

His gaze skimmed her face, lingering on her lips. "For?"

"Being as crazy and impulsive as me."

"I wouldn't go that far." But he was smiling as he stepped away.

Briar watched Vander and Jet do a preflight check and then they were buckled into their seats and Vander was speaking to someone in the tower and they were off.

It didn't even cross Briar's mind until later that it seemed an ungodly hour to have someone in the tiny airport's tower, but soon they were off, up and over the mountains with all the associated turbulence, and then they were above the clouds and the sun was emerging and it was smooth sailing for a couple hours until they neared Las Vegas.

There were a few more bumps on the descent, with Jet glancing back at her a couple times checking in on her. She gave him a thumbs-up because she was doing fine. With the city stretching beneath them, she felt excitement more than fear. They were doing this.

Van had them on the ground taxiing toward the sleek, low terminal and before she knew it, Jet had their bags and they were hugging Van goodbye. Jet said it was his hope they could get out late afternoon, or even early evening, but obviously weather would play a big part.

Vander promised to keep Jet informed and then Jet carried their bags through the small terminal outside to a waiting Uber driver.

As the driver whisked them—well, whisking wasn't truly the word as there was a lot of traffic—to the courthouse. Jet told her after the courthouse they'd go to the hotel where he'd book rooms for the day. He thought Briar should have a room of her own where she could get ready, and maybe even take a nap, as they'd woken up early and it was going to be a long day.

She was touched by his thoughtfulness and realized she knew nothing about how one married in Las Vegas. "So how does this work?" she asked. "Do we just show up somewhere, or do we need appointments?"

Jet laid out the day. Right now, they were on the way to the courthouse where they'd pick up their marriage license. It would be relatively quick since they'd already filled out everything online and paid the fee. After they had the license, there would be a couple hours free before they headed to the chapel.

Briar hadn't realized you couldn't just show up at most chapels and get the deed done. It was big business to marry in Las Vegas and many chapels were booking days, if not weeks, out. Briar tried to picture her dad's face when he learned that she'd married in Las Vegas. It wasn't the wedding he'd wanted for her, and to be fair, she'd always pictured him walking her down the aisle. She pushed the thought away. Life was full of change and not all traditions were meant for everybody.

After the courthouse, they headed to their hotel on the

Strip. The soaring lobby was topped by a glass dome, the dome centered over a tall-built fountain. White marble covered every other surface, from walls to floors to columns. She waited next to Jet while he checked them in, relieved he had booked two hotel rooms, as she suddenly felt strange. Light-headed and shy.

On the twenty-second floor, he walked her to her room, set her bag inside and told her he'd be back at four fifteen to get her for their five o'clock ceremony. She locked the door behind him and then climbed into bed fully dressed, exhausted. It seemed like she'd only just closed her eyes when her alarm sounded, letting her know it was time to get ready.

Briar put her long hair in a scrunchie and then covered it was a shower cap before taking a very fast shower. She'd brought jeans to wear, along with a white billowy blouse, no longer billowy, and her favorite boots. She added a turquoise necklace and her big silver belt buckle from the one barrel-racing event she'd won in high school, and it only fit around her waist on the loosest setting. She tried to position it so that the buckle tipped forward, as if it was a fashion decision. With her long hair loose over her shoulders, she put on a little makeup and looked at her reflection. She hoped Jet wouldn't be disappointed. She looked like she was going to a rodeo after-party not a wedding, but in the end it didn't matter much.

Jet knocked on her door at four fifteen. The man was always on time. She liked that about him. He knew how to be organized. He didn't waste time or play games. She opened the door to him and froze. Jet was wearing a fitted charcoal blazer, a crisp white shirt, dark denims, black boots, and a black Stetson. He, too, was wearing a big shiny silver buckle and with his hair freshly washed and curling a little over the collar of his shirt, she thought he was impossibly handsome.

"This is for you," he said handing her a shopping bag.

"What is it?" she asked, gesturing him in.

He looked almost embarrassed. "I wasn't sure if you'd brought anything special for the ceremony and I saw this downstairs in one of the boutiques. If you don't like it, or it doesn't fit, I can return it later."

"For me to wear today?"

Dark color suffused his cheekbones. "They have a Western store in the lobby. It was on the mannequin in the window. I thought it'd look nice on you. But if it's not your style..." His voice faded.

She pulled the tissue-wrapped skirt from the silver paper bag and held it up, letting it unfold. She didn't know what she'd expected but it wasn't this—a long white skirt, fitted over the hips with ruffles above the knees and that spilled in tiers all the way to the long tail.

It was a very feminine skirt and unlike anything she owned.

"It's a medium," Jet said. "I wasn't sure what size would fit with you being—"

"Pregnant?" she said, smiling mischievously.

"Yeah."

"Let me go try it on."

In the bathroom, she blinked back tears. His thoughtfulness touched her. He'd made an effort today and he'd also thought of her.

The skirt was a little tight on the waist, but she draped her blouse over it and then put the belt on top, the leather band in the low of her back and the buckle positioned on her belly. She adjusted her necklace and then looked at herself in the mirror. She looked like a cowgirl about to get married.

Her eyes smarted and she fought tears, thinking of her mom Joany, wishing she was here, thinking of her dad, wishing he was the one giving her away, but she carried them in her heart and that would have to be enough today.

Leaving the bathroom, she did a little twirl in front of Jet. "It fits," she said. "What do you think?"

"I think you're beautiful," he said, his gaze meeting hers, holding hers, melting her all over again.

"It's the skirt," she said.

"No, it's you. You're beautiful, Briar."

Her cheeks burned hotter, and she gathered a few things for her purse. "I'm ready," she said facing him.

He nodded once. "Let's go."

She'd expected the ceremony to be fast. She hadn't expected all the extra little touches. Jet had made a number of calls, not just reserving the chapel, but ordering flowers, requesting a witness, even booking a photographer—the witness—to take a dozen photos. Briar hadn't understood the reason for photos until Jet murmured that their kids would want to see their wedding pictures one day and it would seem odd if there was nothing to show them.

She pictured life in the future. Jet, her, and children. *This is Mommy and Daddy who got married in Las Vegas. Yes, it was exciting. Yes, it was a special day.*

She looked up at Jet, air catching in her throat. He was so handsome, so thoughtful, so everything she'd waned but didn't think she deserved.

They smiled for the photographer, and then she looked up at Jet and smiled just for him. She saw the moment he felt her smile, saw the flicker of fire before he leaned down to kiss her. The kiss was so full of warmth and light she felt as if she glowed.

By the time the kiss ended, she couldn't help reaching up to touch his cheek, her fingers light on his jaw. He was beautiful and tough. A fighter, a family man, he was hers. Her husband. Her heart. Her future.

After the photos and ceremony, they went into the office and signed the paperwork, and took one last picture of them smiling as they signed. The woman running the office said she would get everything filed, and for them to just enjoy the day. Briar and Jet thanked her, and they left the chapel, husband and wife.

That was that, Briar thought. It was done.

They were married, and just like that she'd become Mrs. Jet Manning.

She thought of her father, thought of her brother, but she didn't feel guilty. This wasn't about them. This wasn't about anyone but Briar and Jet.

Leaving the chapel in the back of a taxi, Jet read a text that made his brow furrow, and she watched his face wondering what had happened.

He didn't leave her waiting. "It's not going to be safe to fly tonight," he said. "Vander doesn't think we'd be able to fly for several days." He put away his phone and looked at her. "The storm is moving in. The airlines serving Wyoming are already canceling flights for the next two days. We can wait it out here or rent a truck and try to make it back before it hits the Sundowner."

She didn't even hesitate. "Let's rent a truck and get on the road as soon as we can."

It took a little over an hour to track down the right truck and collect their things from the hotel, but they were on the road well before dark.

"I'm planning on driving all night," Jet said. "But if the conditions get bad, I'm not going to have us on the road. We'll find a motel somewhere and play it safe."

"I like the sound of that."

"You trust me?"

She couldn't hide her smile. "I married you, Mr. Manning, didn't I?"

It was just after midnight, and they'd made it through Salt Lake City without too much trouble. As they left the city behind, it became dark, no moon or stars, just low heavy clouds. Temperatures had been dropping steadily. As they reached Ogden, tiny bits of ice hit the windshield and Jet periodically turned on the windshield wipers to clear the glass. Fortunately, inside the truck cab it was warm and cozy.

Jet had been wonderful about making frequent stops for her, each break was just long enough for her to use the bathroom and stretch her legs. Dinner was a drive-through burger place, with a celebration cookies and cream milkshake.

They laughed about that. A burger, fries, and milkshake for a wedding dinner. Briar assured him she didn't care. "Not much of a foodie," she confessed. "In fact, if you haven't yet noticed, I like my food rather plain. I don't have adventurous taste buds. Pizza, spaghetti, chicken, steak. Nothing too spicy or exotic for me."

"That's okay, you're spicy enough as it is," he answered, reaching out and taking her hand, lifting her fingers to his mouth. He kissed one finger, and then another even as he kept his attention on the road.

She watched him, not the road. She couldn't wait for the day she could actually, properly touch him. Not necessarily sexually, but to be able to touch his face, his arms, his chest. She wanted to sink into his warmth and feel his arms wrap around her and hold her.

He glanced in her direction even as he put her hand on his thigh. Heat rushed through her; his thigh was hard, taut, sinewy.

"Tell me what you're thinking," he said. "Straight up. Be honest with me."

"Which thought?"

"The one you were thinking just now when I looked at you."

She swallowed hard, wanting to lie but she didn't. "I was thinking about you. Being with you. Not necessarily jumping into sex, but just being close. Being held by you. I was thinking about that."

"Hmm." It was all he said but the awareness in the truck ratcheted up, as if she'd just leaned over and cranked the volume to loud, louder.

His thigh flexed, his body hard, his skin hot. Her hand burned and the heat seeped up her arm into her chest, filling her middle, dancing through her veins. He wanted her, too. She felt it. Knew it. And it made her breathless. Made her want him even more. She'd never been properly loved but maybe Jet would do that. Maybe he'd care for her. Maybe he was the man God made for her.

Jet's hand covered hers on his leg. "Can I ask you about that night with Garrett?"

She sucked in a breath, unsettled. "It's so long ago."

"I just need to understand something. About that night,

how he treated you."

"What do you want to know?" she asked lowly.

"Was it really your first time?"

Briar hesitated and then nodded.

Jet's jaw tightened. Silence stretched. His strong fingers laced between hers, pressing into his thigh.

"You said he wasn't aggressive," Jet added. "Isn't that right?"

She didn't know how to have this conversation when Jet was holding her hand so securely. She felt as if he was holding her on purpose, holding her to keep her from escaping.

She moistened her upper lip. "It was disappointing. He was disappointing. At first, I thought I wanted to … do it … and then I didn't, but by then it was too late. There was no going back and foolish me didn't realize that what I wanted it to be wasn't what it was at all."

"Did you tell him to stop?"

Briar exhaled. "Not quite in those words."

"What words did you use?"

"I don't remember exactly. Something along the lines that this wasn't a good idea after all. That I wasn't sure anymore I wanted to go all the way."

"And what did he say?" Jet replied.

"Not much," she answered, slipping her hand out from beneath his.

It wasn't easy. He didn't want to let her go.

Jet's voice sounded harsh in the dark. "So, it wasn't consensual."

She shrugged unhappily. "I don't know. That's the confusing part. I could have kneed him, you know. I could have shouted at him. I could have made him stop. But I didn't. I thought ... we've gone this far. Let's just get it over with so I can go home."

"And that's what happened?"

"He came and I went." Briar's voice cracked. "That's really the sum of it. It felt empty. I felt empty. I didn't understand why anyone would enjoy that."

Jet turned the windshield wipers up, making them go faster, needing to clear the ice and snow better.

She couldn't look at him, and so she focused on the highway and the swirling snow. "Romance novels make sex sound beautiful and fulfilling. I thought I would feel something. But I didn't. It was just very rough and clinical. Almost like an impatient doctor giving a pelvic exam."

Jet swore beneath his breath. "It could have at least given you pleasure."

She laughed grimly. "You mean, instead of a baby?" Tears filled her eyes, and she impatiently wiped them away. "I don't want to cry. I'm not going to cry. I'm not mad at him, I'm mad at myself."

"You should be mad at him, Briar—"

"No. I'm not blaming others anymore. I realize now how much control I've had. I'm not helpless. I'm not a victim. I made a mistake but that's behind me. I'm determined to be a good mother, and I'll do my best to be a good wife. Garrett doesn't matter. You matter. The baby matters. The rest of it is in the past."

Jet glanced at her, shook his head. "Wow."

"Wow what?"

"You're pretty impressive."

"You're laughing at me," she protested.

"Not at all. I'm impressed. My Briar Phillips—"

"Manning," she corrected.

He grinned. "Briar Phillips Manning is growing up."

She smiled even as she knocked away the remaining tears. "Took long enough, didn't it?"

♥

THE SNOW WAS coming down thicker and thicker. Briar glanced at the clock on the dash. It was a few minutes after four and Jet had driven through the night, driving without complaining but he had to be tired. She saw him blink a couple times in a row and rub his eyes. She couldn't see a lot, and even as a passenger she found it exhausting concentrating on the road. There was so much snow, and the wind was blowing it every which way. She wouldn't call it a blizzard, but it seemed awfully close.

"How are you holding up?" she asked quietly, speaking for the first time since they last stopped to refuel at Kemmerer.

"A little tired but I'm okay."

"You've been up over twenty-four hours now."

The edge of his mouth lifted. "Nothing compared to my Navy training."

"Yes, but we're not preparing for war. Why don't we stop somewhere? Call it a night. You've been amazing, but you've got to be tired. I'm exhausted."

"Only five hours away," he said gruffly.

"Five hours in these conditions feels like fifty. I don't think we should chance it. There's got to be a little town coming up. I don't care where we stay. Let's just find a motel and crash. Even four hours of sleep would be better than nothing."

"We might not be able to drive tomorrow."

She looked out at the white swirling world beyond the glass. It had been a wish to get back quickly, but if it wasn't practical, then so be it. "I know I was the one anxious to be back, but it's silly for me to stress about being gone a second day." She hesitated. "By the way, what did you tell everyone about us going away?"

"I left a note for Cade and Miss Warner that I was taking you to see your father."

Briar's mouth opened and closed. Oh. That was interesting. Hopefully neither of them knew her dad was overseas. "I suppose it'd be hard for Cade to find fault with that."

"Oh, he found fault with it. He called me three times today."

"Three times? Did you ever talk?"

"No. I didn't pick up and haven't listened to his voice mails. I didn't want to let him ruin our wedding day." Jet ran a hand over his jaw, deep creases at the corner of his eyes, the creases illuminated by the dash. "I did want you to see your father today. I called him to invite him to join us."

She turned in the seat, drawing her knees up. "You did?"

"I'd hoped he'd be able to walk you down the aisle."

"Thank you," she whispered, a lump filling her throat.

"He did call me back," Jet said. "But he couldn't make it. He's in Australia. Did you know that?"

"I did. He's doing some work with the rodeo association there."

"Cowboy church?"

"Yes. He invited me to go with him, but I used the opportunity to come to the Sundowner, hoping to have a plan by the time he returned." She studied Jet's profile. "So, he knows we're married?"

"He knows I wanted to marry you today."

"He wasn't happy about it, was he?" she said, hands knotting in her lap.

"He asked if we could wait until he got back, and I said no sir. But I assured him you'd be calling soon, and when you did, you'd tell him everything." Jet looked at her. "I think you should do that sooner than later."

"I will, I promise. Just need a little sleep first."

The next town up was a place called Lander, population

7,550. There were a few motels off the highway but one was dark and the other had a neon sign reading No Vacancy.

Jet took the turnoff for downtown and there was another motel right on Main Street named Frontier Lodge. It was a little place with a huge restaurant sign. Despite the snow, the place was brightly lit and as Jet pulled up front, he shifted into park. "I'll go inside and see if they have a room for us. Stay put and keep warm."

He wasn't gone terribly long, less than ten minutes, and he'd left the truck running and the heater on, but in the time he was gone, snow piled thickly on the windshield making it impossible to see.

Jet returned with a key and a map of Lander. "In case we want to go exploring," he said, handing both to her.

She made a face. "Maybe some other time."

"I agree."

There were parking spots available in front of their room, number nine, and Jet parked the truck and came around to open her door. He scooped her out of the truck and carried her to the motel room's threshold. "We go all out on honeymoons, Mrs. Manning."

Setting her down, he took the key from her and unlocked the door and pushed it open.

It was dark inside and he ran his hand on the wall, feeling for the light switch. Once the light was on Briar saw the room was small and plain, but it looked clean, with two double beds and two pillows on each bed. There was a lamp on a nightstand between the beds, and another old-fashioned lamp on the dresser.

Jet walked into the bathroom and, stepping out, he nodded at her. "It's clean, dry, and once we turn on the heater, it'll be warm."

She turned on the heater while Jet carried their things in from the truck. Once inside, Jet locked the door and disappeared into the bathroom to shower. Briar changed quickly into her pajamas while he showered, the flannel bottoms hugging beneath the swell of her belly, the top one of her dad's old T-shirts, one he'd thrown out years ago that she claimed for herself. It used to be huge on her.

She waited for Jet to emerge from the bathroom. "Which bed?" she asked him, too tired to focus on the fact that there were two beds and not one.

"You take that one," he said, indicating the bed by the bathroom. "I want the bed by the door."

She nodded and disappeared into the bathroom and when she came back, Jet was in his bed, and even though all the lights were still on, he was asleep.

Briar moved around the room turning off the lamps and the overhead light. Then, pausing next to Jet's bed, she looked down at him thinking this was the first time she'd ever seen him sleep. The first time she'd ever seen him not in control.

It made her feel protective and quietly she slipped into her bed and pulled the covers up to her chin.

What a very strange wedding day. It wasn't a bad day. It was just different ... probably not the wedding day most girls dreamed of. Fortunately, Briar wasn't most girls, either.

Chapter Twelve

WHEN BRIAR WOKE up Jet wasn't in his bed. In fact, his bed was neatly made, pillows plumped, bedspread hanging exactly so. The door to the bathroom was open but there was no light on. Sitting up, she looked for his duffel and relaxed when she saw it next to the armchair in the corner. She suspected he'd gone for coffee but just to make sure, she went to the window and moved the curtain at the window. It was good to see his big truck out front, too, even though it was covered in snow, at least a foot or more on the hood and roof.

Dropping the curtain, she used the bathroom and climbed back into bed to stay warm. As she pulled up the covers the baby made a little move of her own and Briar inhaled sharply, and laughed, amazed by the sensations inside of her. Amazed by the baby she carried. Now that she knew she could keep her, and would keep her, Briar felt excited. It would be a huge change this summer, but it would be wonderful. Briar knew she could be a good mom. She'd been raised by a good mom. She could do this.

There were a lot of things that needed to be decided

though. Logistics that she and Jet had not yet discussed.

Like, where would she and Jet live? She couldn't imagine they'd stay as they were, with Jet in the bunkhouse and she up at the main house. She couldn't see Jet up at the main house, either. And as much as Briar adored Miss Warner, Miss Warner's home was not her home.

She and Jet would need to have a conversation about it before they returned to the Sundowner because it would be a question everyone asked.

What was their plan now?

Where would they live?

What would they do?

She heard the key in the door and the motel room door swung open. Jet was carrying a tray with cups on top of two cardboard take-out boxes, his coat and hat dusted in snow. Without missing a beat, he used his foot to close the door.

"Breakfast," he said.

"Thank you." She sat up and shifted the pillows behind her, creating support for her back. "Have you been up long?"

"A half hour or so. Thought I'd find coffee and get some weather reports."

"And?"

"I talked to some of the truckers overnighting here and nothing has been plowed yet. The interstate is a mess. Some folks lost control of their cars and they've abandoned them. Others are stuck inside their cars. Tow-truck drivers can't get to them until the snowplows do their thing." He set the carboard boxes on the nightstand and handed her a steaming cup and kept the extra-large cup for himself. "We're not going anywhere this morning."

"But it's stopped snowing, hasn't it?" she asked, peeking beneath the lid as it didn't smell like her normal tea.

It was hot chocolate with a mountain of melting whipped cream. She smiled, thinking she hadn't had hot chocolate in forever.

"Briefly. It's supposed to snow for the next several days."

"No."

He shrugged. "If it were just me, I might try to make a run for it, but I'm not going to risk your safety. Far better for us to stay warm here, where we have food and entertainment—"

"What entertainment?"

"We have a TV in our room, and the restaurant Maverick's also has a bar, and there's a pool table inside. We won't be bored."

"Question. Were the two beds your idea?" she asked. "Or were the king beds all sold out?"

"My request," he said, taking one of the cardboard boxes to the corner chair. "We both have the same thing. Scrambled eggs, hash browns, bacon, sausage, and toast. There should be a packet of plastic utensils and a ketchup inside the box, too."

Briar didn't care about eggs, the plastic utensils, or a packet of ketchup. She wanted to know why Jet had requested two beds but didn't have the courage. Maybe he'd done it for her. Or maybe he'd done it for himself. Maybe she'd just drink her cocoa and focus on what she'd tell Cade. She'd have to call Cade today. And her father.

Briar let Jet eat, and after a little bit, opened her box and ate some of her eggs and a slice of toast, and then the hash browns which were normally not her favorite but tasted really good. "Have you had any more calls from Cade?" she asked, as she reached for a strip of bacon.

"No. But I sent him a text this morning, and said you were safe, we were together, and due to the storm, we probably wouldn't be back today."

"Did he answer?"

"No."

"I don't really want to talk to him," she said. "He's going to be upset."

"At first, maybe. He's just going to have to get used to things being different. For people like Cade and me, we're people who like control, change takes time. But eventually he'll be fine." He looked at Briar. "Don't let him intimidate you. He's not mean. He's just very protective. That's not a bad thing."

"My parents weren't half as protective as Cade. They let me experiment and be who I wanted to be. I don't think I appreciated it then, but I do now." Briar studied her new husband, realizing it was the first time she'd seen him with scruff.

Every morning he'd always been shaven. When he came to dinner, he'd most likely shaved again. With his dark hair and blue eyes and a shadowed jaw he was very appealing—very, very—and it made her feel a little breathless and light-headed just being here, in the motel room, with him.

He'd almost finished everything in his breakfast box and the way he ate made her almost see who he'd been, when in the Navy, when a pilot, and an officer. "Knowing where you've been, and what you've done, what do you want to do ... in the future? If you could do anything, what would it be?"

Jet closed the lid on the box and set it aside. "Probably what I'm doing now."

"Being a cowboy?"

He laughed, the sound rumbling through his chest, vibrating through her. "I think of myself more as a rancher, but sure, cowboy works."

"Do you want your own place, or do you want to be like Cade and manage someone else's ranch?"

"Cade has it pretty sweet."

"You heard it's all going to be his one day?"

"Yes. Why? Does it bother you?"

"No. I'm glad for him. Miss Warner has been the one person consistently there for him since he was sixteen. They're very close and let's face it, she has no children, so she has to leave it to someone."

"She does have cousins, or distant nieces and nephews,

but I understand they didn't care about her as much as they cared about the inheritance."

Briar thought for a moment. "I don't think Cade cares that much about inheriting. I think he cares about protecting what Miss Warner loves. Continuing her legacy."

"Definitely. Cade isn't materialistic. He's a very hard worker, and a good boss. He's fair—"

"Maybe to his employees."

"I don't think he means to be unfair to you, Briar. I think he's trying to figure out the best way to be a big brother, especially to a firecracker like you."

"Am I a firecracker?"

"You know you are."

She grinned and set her half-eaten breakfast aside on the nightstand next to her half-drunk hot chocolate and drew the sheet and blanket up higher, covering her chest. "You have a really nice way of making my intense personality socially acceptable."

He laughed and extended his legs, crossing one boot over the other. "You are socially acceptable."

"Then why didn't more people want to hire me?" she asked. "In high school, I found it hard to get jobs."

"You needed the jobs?"

"I wanted money of my own. We weren't poor, but we certainly were always careful, especially after Mom was gone. She had a good job and brought in more income than Dad. Without her, it was a struggle, and I did what I could. I cleaned houses, walked dogs, exercised horses. In high school, when I was able to drive, I got my first real job at the Java Café in Marietta, but then lost the job because my Goth persona scared the regulars."

He snorted, trying to hold back laughter. "You went through a Goth phase?"

"Black hair, black eye shadow, black lips, black nails. Probably not the most appetizing face to see first thing in the morning when you're ordering your muffin and coffee."

"Why Goth?"

"I needed to show everyone I was different. I wasn't boring like them."

Jet shook his head. "Why do I feel like our little girl is going to be a handful?"

Briar held her breath, eyes stinging, emotion filling her. *Our little girl.* She blinked and smiled unsteadily. "Thank you," she said huskily.

"For?"

She struggled to hold back the tears. "For being you."

JET CLEARED AWAY their breakfast things, taking the garbage outside to the dumpster in the back. It meant walking through wet powdery snow, but his boots and jeans kept his feet dry, and the cold fresh air helped clear his head.

He'd offered to marry Briar for the reasons he told her—it was something he could do that would help her. It would mean she could keep her daughter. He would be able to provide for both of them and protect them, but he wasn't selfless or altruistic. He'd also married her because she was beautiful and smart, as well as funny, complex, layered, interesting. She was the first woman he'd met who made him want to know more, and the more he learned, the more he liked her. Admired her. If he was going to marry, she would be the one. She should be the one. He didn't know why and he couldn't explain it, but he felt most like himself when with her. He felt like the man his mother had raised. He felt like the boy he'd once been, looking up at the stars with her as she showed him all the different constellations and the stories associated with them.

He'd inherited his ability to dream from her. He'd learned how to work hard from her. And even though he had spent years refusing to feel, he did have a heart, and he loved because of her. His mother had been a wonderful person. They hadn't needed money. They had each other.

Her death had broken an important piece of him, and he hadn't thought he'd ever recover, not emotionally, but somehow Briar had helped heal that piece, and he wasn't sure if it was her fierceness or her irreverence or her struggle to do what was right, despite the pressure on her. But her struggle to be real, to be honest, to be true, to be herself resonated with him.

One day, he'd have to tell her that he hadn't married her to be a good person. He hadn't married her to be a hero.

He'd married her because she somehow had rescued him. And he hadn't even known he needed saving.

Back in the room, he discovered Briar had turned the TV on and was watching the news. He eased his wet boots off, placed them before the floor heater, and changed in the bathroom into sweatpants.

"You're right," she said to him as he opened the door and laid his wet jeans over the heat. "It's going to snow for the next twenty-four hours."

He drew back the covers of his bed and climbed in, propping himself up as Briar had done. "At least they have a restaurant here and the manager said they intend to keep it open. They have plenty of food, but they are down a cook and wait staff."

They watched TV until noon when Briar began to seem restless, and Jet suggested they check out the restaurant and bar. They bundled up and walked the short distance to the restaurant, which anchored the motel complex.

It had started to snow again while they'd been inside, and despite the thick white flurries, a half-dozen people were in the restaurant, a few at the counter, others at tables. The menu was limited due to the staffing issues but there was homemade chicken soup and toasted turkey and swiss cheese sandwiches. They ate and Briar talked, making observations about their fellow diners. She was very imaginative and had stories for each of them. He listened, amused, content to just look at her and nod when necessary.

She was so pretty and expressive, too. He liked just watching her, listening to her, as her hands gestured as she talked, and her green eyes were bright with humor, her lovely lips curving with laughter. Now that she felt safe, she was opening up and revealing more of herself and she had a really good brain and a big personality and he hoped that her baby, their baby, would be like her. If only more people were like her.

Briar abruptly stopped talking and stared at the man who'd just entered the restaurant. Jet looked from Briar to the man, and he knew what she was thinking, but she was wrong. It wasn't Garrett. It just looked like him.

She came to the same conclusion and looked at Jet, the laughter gone, lips compressed. "I thought…"

"I know," Jet said. "There is a similairy."

"How do you know?"

"I looked him up, studied him a bit, just in case."

She arched an eyebrow, the teasing light returning to her eyes. "In case you wanted to spend more time in jail?"

He shook his head, but he couldn't help smiling. She was sassy and bold and brave and exactly what he wanted. Exactly who he needed.

Jet hadn't thought he'd ever marry and now that he had, he was glad. There would be issues and struggles but he wasn't worried. There were things they needed to decide, but they had time. Some decisions couldn't be made until after they returned to the Sundowner.

He wondered if Briar had thought about the future, and where they'd go, because they weren't going to be able to stay on the ranch, he was fairly certain of that. If there was available housing that would be one thing, but the bunkhouse was for bachelors, Cade and MerriBee had the original homestead, and Miss Warner had the big house, which also accommodated Willis and Emma as they had their own apartment. Short of moving in with Miss Warner—which he didn't consider an option—they'd have to find their own place elsewhere. That also meant he might need to find work elsewhere. Jet didn't typically stay in one place long, so it wasn't a problem for him, but he didn't know about Briar.

After lunch they wandered to the bar, and seeing that no one was at the pool table, Briar challenged him to a game.

"You play?" he asked.

"Of course. All pastors' daughters do." Then she winked.

He shouldn't have been surprised then that she was good. They spent an hour playing, game after game, and Briar won at least half of them. His new wife was a woman of hidden talents. He wondered what else she was good at. He looked forward to finding out.

Briar suddenly yawned and smiled sheepishly. "I'm still tired."

"You only slept a couple hours."

"It was more than that. It had to be at least four."

"Not enough," he said, retrieving their coats. "Let's head back. I'd love a nap."

But once back in their room, Jet was on his phone trying to get updates on the weather, especially north near the Sundowner.

Briar, back in her pajamas, tried to sleep but tossed restlessly. After twenty minutes she sat up. "I need to call them. I don't think I should wait. I don't want anyone to worry. I will feel better once I talk to Dad and break the news to Cade." She shot Jet a troubled look. "I really hate disappointing people."

"You're an adult. You have your own life. They'll both be fine."

Briar hesitated. "What time do you think it is in Australia?"

"Morning. Probably early. Six, maybe seven."

"He'd be awake," she said. "Dad's an early riser." Then she drew a deep breath and called her dad's number. Jet heard Patrick answer.

"Dad, it's me," Briar said, her voice unsteady. "How are you?"

Jet listened to Briar tell her dad nearly everything. That she was pregnant, and she'd just gotten married in Las Vegas to Jet Manning. She said she hadn't known that Jet invited her dad, but she was glad he'd thought of that. She wished her father could have been there and that she loved him and when he was home she'd come see him.

She stopped talking then, and for a long minute she was silent, just listening to her father.

Jet couldn't hear what Patrick was saying. Her eyes filled with tears, and she took a quick breath and then another.

Jet left his bed and went to sit beside her.

She glanced at him and struggled to smile. "Dad," she said, still looking at Jet. "He wasn't the one who got me pregnant, but he's going to be the dad. She's due—"

Her father said something, and Briar wiped away a tear.

"Yes, Dad. I'm having a little girl. She should be here around July second, and I know this is a lot to take in, but it's going to be okay. We're going to make this work. Please don't worry."

The call ended not long after and Briar inhaled and exhaled. "One down, one to go."

"How did he react?" Jet asked.

"He was calm, as always." Her voice dropped, deepening. "He said he was sorry I'd been dealing with this on my own, and that he's looking forward to being a grandfather. He does love kids."

"Do you feel better?"

She nodded. "Yes." She sniffled. "Now it's just Cade I have to tell. But I don't think he'll take it as well."

Jet leaned forward and kissed her forehead. "It's really none of his business, and if he gets in your face, I don't have a problem telling him so."

She put a hand to his chest and pushed him back and looked him in the eye. "Don't get into it with Cade," she pleaded, "not because of me. He could fire you—"

"He won't."

"He could."

Jet shrugged. "Then we go somewhere else. I'm not worried. You're my first priority, not him."

She ducked her head. "I don't think I should return with you to the Sundowner. I think it's just going to make everything harder, mostly for you. Cade is not going to be happy. And I can't see him letting me move into the bunkhouse with you."

"No, he won't," Jet agreed. "But we also don't have to have a permanent solution the moment we return. We can adjust and be flexible. Having a temporary plan isn't the end of the world."

"I stay up at the house, and you're still down in the bunkhouse?"

"It would give us time to come up with a better plan."

She bit into her lower lip, expression pensive. He knew this wasn't a great plan, but it gave everyone at the Sundowner time to adjust.

"I don't want to be alone," she said. "I'm tired of doing this alone."

"I'll be there—"

"On the ranch, with Cade, or talking to Miss Warner about hay."

Jet fought his smile, knowing Briar wouldn't appreciate it, but she was funny, and even when she was being dramatic, she made him laugh. "You do know what temporary means?" he said, lifting a long silky strand of hair from her cheek, and smoothing it behind her ear.

"It's just that I lived with this secret for so long. It's worn me down. You make me feel strong."

"Because you are strong."

He reached for her hand, and brought it to his mouth, kissing the clenched fist. "Don't stress. It's not worth it. We're in this together. You're stuck with me now whether you like it or not."

That made her smile and she looked into his eyes. "I have to know something."

"Okay."

"Why did you get separate beds?"

"Because I want you to feel comfortable—"

"I do."

"We will have forever now. There's no need for us to rush things." He pried open her fist and kissed each fingertip before placing a kiss to the middle of her palm. "I've never been able to woo you properly. Now I can."

She frowned. "You don't have to woo me. You've won me. Surprise! I'm yours."

He couldn't ever remember smiling this much. "Do you want me to make love to you?"

"Yes." And then she turned pink. "I mean, you kiss really well—like really, really well—and I just want everything else with you."

"I don't want to hurt you, or the baby."

"You won't." Her frown was back. "At least, I don't think you will. I haven't investigated it that much. There's been other things to worry about."

"And there are still other things to worry about, which is why for now, sex and orgasms will have to wait—" He broke off when she blushed furiously again. "Does that embarrass you?"

"No." She cleared her throat. "Yes. But it's not just that. It's, well, you're kind of turning me on."

Jet kissed her then, a deep hungry kiss that made him hard and ache. Her mouth was soft and hot and sweet. She felt like his, and he knew he'd do anything for her, that he'd die for her, that she was the reason he was still on earth.

For Briar and Briar's little girl. Their little girl.

Reluctantly he ended the kiss. Her mouth looked swollen and lush. He wanted to taste that mouth again, but was afraid if he continued kissing her, he'd be touching her, and he had willpower but he was also a man.

"Call your brother," he said hoarsely, leaving the side of her bed. "I'm going to go buy us some bottles of water. Text me when you're done. I want to give you privacy and space."

"Jet," she said, voice quivering as he put his coat on.

He turned at the door to face her.

"I appreciate you giving me privacy now," she said. "But I don't want any more nights alone. My thoughts overwhelm me. I become afraid." She swallowed and tried to smile but failed. "I just want everyone to know. I want to move past this part where it's nerve wracking and scary. I need to feel safe."

"You are safe." His gaze searched hers. "You will always be safe with me."

"Then let's make a pact that we stay together. I don't want anyone to come between us. I don't want anyone to threaten you—"

"No one will threaten me," he assured her, returning to her side, and lightly touching her cheek. "No one is going to intimidate you. Just call your brother. Get this over with—"

She caught his hand, held it tightly. "He's afraid I'm too much like our mom. He's afraid I'm wild like her."

"I don't get that from him at all. Cade has strong opinions, but he has tremendous integrity. He's a very straight-up guy. No games. No bullshit. Briar, you'll feel better after you've spoken to him. Fear of the unknown is far worse than the truth."

He gave her hand a squeeze and left the motel room before he climbed in bed with her and comforted her the best way he knew how.

Chapter Thirteen

Briar clutched her phone as the door closed behind Jet.

She hadn't wanted him to go, but at the same time, she thought it was better he wasn't here to overhear the conversation. It might not be pleasant, regardless of what Jet thought.

Gathering her courage, she phoned Cade, and he answered on the first ring.

"Where have you been?" he demanded.

And just like that her temper flared and, instead of being calm and conciliatory, she flashed right back. "Let's see. Yesterday it was Las Vegas, around midnight it was Salt Lake City and this morning it's Lander."

"I don't need the sarcasm. I've been worried sick."

Some of her anger deflated. "I'm not trying to upset you, Cade, but you talk to me like I'm fifteen and I've stolen Miss Warner's truck."

"You left no note."

"Jet said he did."

"Jet doesn't work here any longer."

"Cade."

"I'm serious. He's fired."

"Cade."

"He knew the rules. He flagrantly broke the rules—"

"I'm pregnant." She waited a moment, aware that she had her brother's attention now. "Jet married me because I didn't want to place my baby for adoption. I knew you'd think it was the best choice—"

"I'd never pressure you into that, Briar."

"But you're always saying how I'm just like Mom." Her voice broke. "I'm not just like Mom. I'm me. And I might look like Mom but I'm more like my mom Joany than Suzy. I'm more like Patrick than you. I'm not a bad person—"

"I never said you were."

"But you've made me feel like a bad person from the very first day you met me and it's not right because you've never given me a chance. You've never gotten to know me."

"That's not true."

"Then why didn't you ever come see me when you visited the Wyatts? Our place is practically on the way. Why didn't you ever drive over just to spend time with me? Why did I no longer matter?"

Cade had no answer and Briar, who'd held all of her fears and hurt and pain in, couldn't keep it to herself anymore. This was her brother. This was supposed to be her family. Where was the love? Where was the support?

"Don't make me pick between you and Jet," she said,

"because I've made my choice. I love Jet. I feel safe with him. I'm happy with him. I feel hope, and I haven't felt hope in forever." And then she hung up because if she was going to lose it, she wasn't going to sob while on the line with her brother.

Briar wept into her pillow for long exhausting minutes. She only stopped crying when she realized she was supposed to text Jet and let him know when she was off the phone.

She was off the phone, but she didn't want him to see her like this. Briar dragged herself into the shower and washed her hair with the shampoo she'd brought with her. The motel room didn't have a blow dryer and she'd forgotten to bring one, so after blotting as much water from her hair as possible, she put her pajamas back on, and climbed back into bed and went to text Jet when she saw she'd missed an incoming text. Well, there were two, actually.

The first was from Miss Warner. *Don't worry about anything, Briar. Life has a funny way of working out. See you soon and give my best to Jet.*

Briar blinked and sniffled, touched and grateful. Miss Warner had never texted her before and it was very sweet of her to text now. Miss Warner also could only know the news because Cade had probably stormed in and told her. Briar wished she'd been the one to tell Miss Warner but what was done was done.

The second text was from MerriBee. *Congratulations, Briar! So happy for you. Can't wait to celebrate with you and Jet once you're home.*

Touched by MerriBee's warmth and kindness, Briar lay back into her pillows and holding her phone against her chest, she tried to focus on the well wishes and not Cade's anger. Still holding the phone, she fell asleep.

BRIAR WAS STILL sleeping when Jet returned and woke her up.

"If we want to try to make it back," he said, "we should leave now. They've plowed Main Street and there's a lane clear on the highway. I think we should go for it. Between my four-wheel drive and the snow tires, we should be in good shape."

Groggy, Briar just looked up at Jet, trying to sort her thoughts. She wasn't at all sure that jumping in the truck was the thing to do. For one, it was still snowing, and for another, back meant the Sundowner and that was the last place she wanted to go right now.

"Maybe we should stay here for another night," she said.

"The wind has died down. It's snowing but conditions are pretty good. Some of the truckers have pushed on and if they can do it, I think we can, too."

"Or we stay here tonight and play more pool."

He pulled the covers off of her. "Or we could start driving and be home in four hours. We'd miss dinner but there might be some dessert left."

She gave him her hand so he could pull her up. "I do like

dessert, especially if it's pie."

"What's your favorite?"

"Any fruit pie. I like them all. Especially with a scoop of ice cream."

"Good girl, so do, I." He unplugged her phone charger, handed her her phone and looked around for anything that still needed packing. "Use the bathroom if you need to, and then we're gone."

They were off soon, too, and it was snowing but it wasn't too bad, the flakes big and white, a slow lazy tumble from the sky. Since it was only four, they still had several hours of daylight left. And if conditions held they'd be back at the ranch around eight since Jet was making good time at the moment.

Briar watched the snow fall, and tried not to think about Cade or how things would be once they returned. Would Cade really fire Jet? Would Miss Warner let him do that to him … to them?

She chewed on her lip, trying not to be anxious anymore. Not wanting to be anxious anymore. She was sick and tired of stress and worry, of guilt and shame. She didn't want to feel like a failure anymore, and she wasn't a failure. Briar knew she was capable and she could work hard and she didn't give up once she was committed, which was why she dreaded returning to the ranch. It wasn't a bad place for others, but it wasn't home, and it would never be her place. She'd always be a guest there and that wasn't how she wanted to start married life.

"Cade's not going to be angry when we arrive. He's going to have had time to think about it and he'll be calm," Jet said, glancing at her. "I've known him over a year now and he isn't one to fume or rage or hold a grudge. That's just not him."

"That's good." She struggled to smile. "I'll just feel better when this part is all done, and everyone knows, and everyone can just be ... kind."

"What else?" he asked, taking her hand.

"What else what?" she answered, liking the way he held her hand, like the feel of his skin against hers, liking how calm he made her feel, how peaceful.

"What else would make you feel better? Be honest. Let's lay all our cards on the table. We can't move forward without knowing what's important to each other."

"Okay," she said, drawing a breath. "I wish we had a little place for us. I'd feel better that way."

He didn't even hesitate. "We can do that."

"Can we?"

His thumb turned the gold band on her ring finger. "Things will be tight financially for a little bit, but we can make it work."

The ring still felt new, but he didn't. Jet felt like everything she loved best. "You've already done so much—"

"Married you in Vegas? Honeymooned in Lander?" He laughed. "Come on, I've done nothing but steal the prettiest girl in all of Montana and Wyoming and make her my wife."

Heat rushed through her, heat and pleasure and the feeling that maybe finally everything was coming together for good. And the good wasn't just for her, or the baby, but for all of them. Maybe her mom was up there above, acting as an angel, being the choir director she used to be, moving all the pieces around until she'd gotten Briar and Jet in the same place together so they could find each other and come together, a new family. Of course, it was just a story, Briar's active imagination, but the idea comforted her. It made her happy.

She looked at Jet, and just looking at him her heart skipped a beat and everything in her felt hopeful. Lucky. "Can we talk about practical stuff?"

"I wish we would," he answered, releasing her hand to turn down the radio.

"Do you pay rent at the ranch?" she asked.

"No, room and board is covered but I have some money, savings from when I was in the Navy."

"But that's yours," she said firmly.

"It's ours," he corrected. "It's there for when we need it. So what else do you want to know?"

"Do you intend to continue working at the Sundowner?"

"It's been a good fit for me. I hadn't intended to leave anytime soon."

"But you will leave eventually?"

He hesitated. "I tend to move around a bit. Not sure

why." He glanced at her. "I'm aware that I can't drag you across the country just because I start to get restless."

"I wouldn't mind. I get restless, too."

"What makes you restless?" he asked.

That was a good question, one she hadn't really thought deeply on. "I've outgrown my dad's home. It is his home, and not mine, not anymore."

"I'm sure he doesn't feel that way."

"I'm not so sure," Briar answered thinking about his trip to Australia and Della, the very pretty barrel racer, a widow who'd lost her husband five years ago in a freak rodeo accident. She was on the trip to Australia. Della was a woman of faith and Briar knew Della and her father had grown close. Briar's father was older, by ten or more years, but after a certain point, age didn't matter. "There could be someone for him, someone he could make a life with, if he didn't have to worry about me."

Jet shot her a glance, intrigued. "You really think so?"

"She's on the trip to Australia. She's a nationally ranked barrel racer. She hasn't been to the NFR since her husband died, but she's still competing on the circuit and making money."

"And you think your dad likes her?"

"They've become close. She's always at the morning prayer breakfasts and sometimes he has her come to the house for dinner. He said she was there to help share her horse knowledge with me, but she and I would talk for a half hour and then they'd be in the kitchen or living room for hours, talking and talking."

"It doesn't make you jealous?"

"No. It makes me happy. Dad is my favorite person," she said making a face at Jet. "Well, he was my favorite person until I met you."

☙

THE SNOW GREW thicker as they approached the Big Horn Mountains, but they'd made good time until now, and so even though Jet had slowed, they should still reach the Sundowner before nine.

On the outskirts of Buffalo Jet pointed out the exit for the property Miss Warner had just bought. "That entire area is now Miss Warner's. Some of the best hay acreage in Wyoming."

"I don't know how Cade is going to manage the Sundowner, which is vast, the summer dude ranch which always sells out, and a new farm," she answered, looking out the window at snow covered fields.

"Willis is in charge of the dude ranch program. Cade runs the ranch proper. If I'm here, I'd like to take on the new farm, but if I'm here Cade will hire someone else."

It was on the tip of her tongue to tell Jet that Cade had threatened to fire Jet, but somehow, she couldn't share that with him. If Cade was truly going to do that, better he do it when Jet and Briar were together because then she'd tell him what she thought of him. She'd tell him how he didn't want to be anything like his stepdad Jimmy but apparently he didn't need the DNA to become an ass—

"What's firing you up?" Jet asked, his hand on her knee. "You look spitting mad."

"Just preparing myself for battle," she answered, covering his hand with hers. "I haven't been to bootcamp and I'm not great at taking orders, but no one is going to mess with you, Jet, not while I'm around."

Jet laughed, and laughed some more, laughing until his tears shone in his eyes, making his black lashes wet. "You don't have to defend me, babe. I can handle myself."

"I know," she said, gently patting his hand. "And I'm not defending you, Jet Manning, I'm protecting what's mine."

❦

THE MAIN HOUSE at the Sundowner was ablaze with lights when Jet pulled into the drive, parking in front of the door. Miss Warner was usually in bed by now, and the house should have been dark, but from the look of it, Miss Warner hadn't gone to bed and was still waiting up.

Jet and Briar exchanged glances, both aware that this wasn't the norm. "Want to come in?" Briar asked him, giving his hand a squeeze, hoping he'd say yes.

He leaned toward her and kissed her, smiling into her eyes. "What a great idea, Briar, thank you for the invite."

"You say that now," she muttered.

He came around, opened her door, helped her out. "Watch the ice," he said. "Looks like Willis salted the pavement but—"

"I'm a Big Sky girl, Jet. I'm familiar with ice."

Jet pocketed his keys and took her hand, walking her to the door. "Who do you think is waiting for us?" he asked, as they reached the front step.

"Everybody? But probably not Grace."

"Or Rolly, Brent, and Ace," Jet added opening the front door for her. "That would be awkward."

She smothered her giggle, grateful for his humor. Tiptoeing she led the way through the entry past the dining room, heading for Miss Warner's family room and, yes, there Miss Warner was, sitting in her chair, watching TV, the sound muted.

"We're back," Briar said loudly, and Miss Warner startled and turned, her pale eyes searching Briar's face and then Jet's.

Briar went to Miss Warner's side and kissed her cheek. "You didn't need to stay up," she said. "It's late for you."

"I'm ninety, not dead," Miss Warner flashed, slowly trying to rise.

"Don't get up," Jet answered, bringing a chair forward for him, and gesturing for Briar to sit in the armchair next to Miss Warner, the one she usually sat in during their evening TV hour.

"Where is everyone else?" Briar asked, taking her familiar

seat.

"In their beds, I'd imagine. I hope they're not here." Miss Warner's tone was tart and she had spots of color high in her cheeks.

"Cade told you," Briar said, leaning forward to be closer to Miss Warner. "I'd hoped to tell you myself."

Miss Warner's fingers drummed on the blanket covering her legs. "As you know, Cade's not happy, but he'll get over it. I think he just needs time to process it." She turned her attention to Jet. "And it's not your baby, is it?"

Jet shook his head. "No, ma'am. I didn't make the baby, but I am going to be her daddy."

Miss Warner's expression softened as she glanced at Briar. "A girl?"

Briar nodded. "She's due early July."

"This is all quite surprising," Miss Warner said.

"I know." Briar hesitated, unsure how to proceed, wanting to be respectful, aware that Miss Warner was raised in a different era with different morals and values. "I'm sorry if I've disappointed you—"

"Why would you disappoint me?" Miss Warner interrupted.

"I can't imagine you approve. I show up at your door young and pregnant."

Miss Warner impatiently waved her hand. "I've always thought it most unfair that women get left with the burden of pregnancy and childcare while men go off free as a bird to do their own thing. Pregnancy and childbirth is not to be taken lightly. Birth is a miracle, but it is also still dangerous. My mother died in childbirth, which is why I was the last of her children. So no, I do not fault you for being young or pregnant, and I think it's remarkable that you and Jet have chosen to move forward together. It makes me respect the two of you more. So, what is your plan now? Where do you intend to stay? It can't be comfortable with you here, and Jet in the bachelor bunkhouse and Cade huffing and puffing over in the homestead."

Briar exchanged amused glances with Jet, determined not to laugh out loud at the description of Cade huffing and puffing as if a wolf trying to blow the little piggies' house down.

"We've agreed to keep things the same for now," Jet said, speaking for both of them, "but we'd like to find ourselves a place of our own. Hopefully close to the ranch so I can continue here."

"Jet likes it here," Briar added.

"But you'd leave here, would you?" Miss Warner asked, focused on Jet. "Find work elsewhere?"

"Only if that became necessary," Jet answered. "I've enjoyed my time here. I've learned a great deal and feel tremendous loyalty to you and Cade."

"Not that much loyalty if you'd marry Briar behind his back," Miss Warner said tartly.

"If it were you, what would you do?" he replied, putting

the ball in her court.

"Exactly what you did. I'm not upset with either of you." She paused and looked at Briar. "I can't believe you've been pregnant this entire time. Where are you hiding that baby?"

Briar blushed and unzipped her vest and patted her middle. "Here. She's sleeping now, but she'll be kicking me later."

"A spirited little thing," Miss Warner said. "I like that. Be sure you teach her to ride. Get her on a horse young."

Briar rose and gave Miss Warner a hug. "Thank you. I know you don't like flattery, but you must know I think you're wonderful."

"I know." Miss Warner patted Briar's back. "You and me, we understand each other, and that's a good thing."

As Briar drew back, Miss Warner carefully got to her feet. "I see it's almost ten. Way past my bedtime." She looked at Jet and held out a hand to him. "Come here."

Jet approached and took her hand.

She held it firmly and gazed into his eyes. "Your Briar is an exceptional young woman and you couldn't have picked a better woman to be your partner in life. Be friends. Treat each other with respect. Keep your sense of humor. And the love will come."

"Yes, ma'am," Jet said, voice deep.

"And one more thing," Miss Warner said as she took her first steps from the room. "I think it's best for you to move upstairs with Briar. Normally as a couple, you'd have a larger room, but her room should suffice for now. You'll have some privacy since it doesn't seem like you had much of a honeymoon."

Chapter Fourteen

The four-poster bed in Briar's room had felt enormous for her, but now that Jet was in it, too, there didn't seem to be that much space.

Jet had fallen asleep almost the moment he'd climbed into bed, but Briar had spent the past hour punching her pillows, turning from one side to another, holding her breath, trying to relax and she was even more awake than she had been earlier.

"Jet?" she whispered.

He said nothing.

"Jet," she said more loudly.

"Hmm?" he answered sleepily.

"I can't sleep."

"Try to count sheep, Briar. One, two, three—"

"It doesn't work, it never has."

He yawned and turned toward her, his hand brushing her shoulder. "Why can't you sleep?"

"Too much on my mind. How can you sleep?"

"Because I'm tired."

She sighed and flipped over on her back. "I wish I was

tired. I don't know why I'm not. I keep thinking about everything—the wedding, the snow, the motel in Lander, the drive here ... talking to Miss Warner. It's been a wild forty-eight hours."

He yawned again. "I don't think it's even been forty-eight hours. It will be soon, so close your eyes and stop thinking."

She closed her eyes and tried hard not to think but all she could see in her mind was Miss Warner and then she pictured Cade and she wondered why MerriBee was so fond of him. Cade was not that likable.

"You're still thinking," Jet said, voice deep and raspy.

And sexy. He had a very sexy voice. "I know," Briar answered, turning again so she could face him. With her cheek on her pillow, she could just make out Jet's profile in the dark. She loved his face. She loved him. She wished she could tell him.

He lightly stroked her arm, his hand warm. "I could tell you about mathematical theories if you'd like. It might help you relax."

She liked the way he touched her. She liked the way he teased her. He made her feel special. Beautiful. She'd waited her entire life to feel this way. "You mean bore me to sleep?"

"Pretty much."

Briar snorted then paused and asked, "Do you know mathematical theories?"

"Of course I do. I'm a math and science geek."

She rolled her eyes. "That explains everything."

He laughed, too, a low, husky sound that made her melt.

"Come closer," he said, lifting the covers up. "Let me explain my world to you. There are hundreds of math theorems," he added, wrapping his arm around her, her back pressed to his chest, his hand on her abdomen. "You can find a list of notable theorems on Wikipedia. Most are pure mathematics but there are some from economics, theoretical physics, and other fields. Abel's theorem on algebraic curves is one of my favorites. Let me explain it to you."

He was still talking when she fell asleep.

SHE WAS ASLEEP. Jet smiled and carefully shifted her in his arm, not wanting to wake her. She was exhausted and needed her rest, but as he eased his arm, his palm resettling on her belly he felt a movement beneath his palm, a fleeting pressure pushing back.

Was that the baby?

Had she just kicked his hand?

Jet swallowed, warmth suffusing his chest. He didn't know how it happened, he who didn't love, loved, and he who didn't feel, felt everything again. He didn't know how it happened, but after years of being alone, he'd finally found home.

Wherever Briar was, that was where he wanted to be. A husband, a father, his family.

Briar woke up slowly, emerging from a lovely dream. She felt good and comfortable, so comfortable. She sighed and snuggled deeper into the covers and then encountered an arm. A warm, very muscular arm. She opened her eyes and looked into Jet's blue eyes.

"Uh, hi," she said, pushing long tangled hair back from her face.

"Hi."

"I forgot about you."

He lifted a dark eyebrow as he peeled hair from her face. "Already?"

She giggled. "I mean, I forgot I scooted toward you."

"Lesson learned, too," he said sternly. "You took it over. Left almost no room for me." But there were creases at the corner of his eyes, and his lips were curving.

Her heart tumbled, a fall through her chest. If she hadn't already known she was crazy about him, she would have figured it out right then.

Downstairs, Cade and MerriBee, along with toddler Grace, were all at the breakfast table with Miss Warner. They seemed to be lingering over their coffee and it crossed Briar's mind as she and Jet entered the room that they'd been waiting for them to appear.

Briar went to Miss Warner and kissed her cheek. "Good

morning," she said.

She then went to MerriBee and gave her a little hug and smacked her lips against Grace's cheek making her laugh before going to the kitchen to get some tea.

Jet joined her and poured himself coffee. "I feel like we're watching a Western drama," he said. "Like *Yellowstone* or *Stardust Ranch* with Max Russo."

"*Stardust* has less violence than *Yellowstone*," she said. "Let's pretend it's that show."

They returned to the table with their coffee and Jet held her chair as she sat down.

"How did everyone sleep?" Briar asked, glancing around the table, feeling the tension but not about to acknowledge it. "I did."

MerriBee smiled at Briar. "I'm glad," she said. "You need the rest. Speaking of which, congratulations, Briar, and welcome to the family, Jet. What an exciting few days it's been for you."

"It has been," Jet agreed, drinking his coffee. "Thank you. We appreciate the support."

Cade made a rough sound and pushed his plate away.

MerriBee flushed. "And I'd love to see your pictures when you have a chance," she added brightly. "I'm just sorry to have missed the wedding." And then, with another smile, she rose and picked Grace up, lifting her from the high chair and walking out.

Emma suddenly appeared in the dining room. "I thought

I heard your voice, Briar. Welcome home. I've heard the news. I think we need a special dinner—"

"Can we wait on that?" Cade interrupted. "I'd like to speak to my sister and Jet before we start making plans."

Emma nodded and left the room but not before everyone caught a glimpse of her crushed expression.

Briar was the first to speak. "What's wrong with you?" she said to Cade, leaning across the table, looking him square in the eyes. "Why can't you be happy for me? For us?"

"You should have told me, Briar. If you needed help, you should have come to me."

"So you could chew me out? Tell me how I'm young and wrong, impulsive and impossible?"

"I've never said those things to you."

"No," she said, rising, "you just can't stop comparing me to your mom. But I'm not Suzy. I'm Briar and I know who I am and know what I need. So, get off your high horse and be the brother I want to love, and if you can't do that, then I don't want to be here. Correction, I don't belong here." Briar drew a deep breath and suddenly she deflated. "I don't belong here, do I?"

She glanced at Miss Warner, tears in her eyes. "Thank you for everything you've done for me, Miss Warner, but it's time I left. I hate leaving today this way but it's time, and I know you'll understand."

NOT YET FINISHED with Cade or his coffee, Jet watched Briar rush out of the dining room, before turning to look at Cade. "Looks like we're leaving after breakfast," he said evenly. "I am sorry that I won't be able to give notice as I never like to leave an employer in the lurch—"

"You're enjoying this," Cade gritted.

"I'm not. But Briar is obviously unhappy and it's time for us to go."

"This isn't a game. She is my family."

"Mine, too," Jet answered. "I love Briar. Nobody's going to mess with her, not even you, big brother."

Miss Warner glanced from one to the other. "I have work to do at my desk. Good day, gentlemen. And should you come to blows, please, take it outside. I don't want anything broken or blood on my carpets."

They both rose, standing as she made her way out.

Cade dropped back into his seat after she'd gone. "This is all your fault."

Jet didn't sit back down. He folded his napkin and prepared to walk out. "I'm not going to argue. I respect Briar too much to fight with you."

"Does she know who you are? Who you really are?" Cade demanded.

"Does she know I'm a felon convicted of assault? Yes. Does she know I served in the US Navy? Yes. Does she know I was raised by a single mom? Yes. Does she know I went after the bastard who murdered my mom—"

"So, she does know what she's getting into. That when you leave here, you'll find it difficult to get another job, that future employers will want to know about your experience, as well as your record."

Jet shook his head. "I have defended you to her again and again, but not anymore. If you want to be an ignorant, prejudiced fool, go right ahead."

"Prejudiced, how?"

"How old was your mom when she had you, Cade? Twenty-one, twenty-two?" He didn't wait for a response. "She was single, too, wasn't she? She married Jimmy because she was young and alone with a baby and it was hard. She struggled to make ends meets. Jimmy seemed like a good answer, but he wasn't, was he? But Briar isn't your mother, and I'm not Jimmy. I love your sister. I would do anything for her, unlike you, who just judges her and punishes her with your constant, endless disapproval."

"It's not like that."

"No? Then how is it?"

Cade looked away, jaw tight. "You should have come to me when you knew her situation. I would have handled this—"

"You have a wife and a baby. What would you have done? How would you have advised her? Would you have wanted her to keep the baby, or would you have encouraged her to place the baby up for adoption?"

"That's not the point. We had a deal—"

Jet shook his head. "We didn't have a deal. There were no deals being made. We did have an understanding initially, but the situation changed, and Briar needed me."

"Whose baby is it?"

"She's mine now, so either support Briar or leave her alone." Jet rose. "I'm not having you upset her, not anymore."

Cade was on his feet, too. "You have no right to tell me anything—"

"I have no right?" Jet took a step toward Cade, closing the distance. "I'm her husband. It gives me a heck of a lot more say than you."

"But you know who the father is," Cade said stubbornly. "Don't you?"

"I do, but why does it matter? How would the knowledge help you? What would you do? Hunt him down, teach him a lesson?"

"I'd like to look the rat in the eye and let him feel my rage."

"That's the problem, Hunt. This isn't about you. It's about Briar. For twenty-eight weeks she's struggled alone trying to figure out what to do, and now when she's finally happy, you want to make her suffer? No."

"Do you really love her? Or is this part of your charade?"

"It doesn't matter. I'm going to take care of her, and that's all that matters. I'll be there in ways you won't—"

"No," Briar said quietly, firmly, entering the dining

room. Color stained her cheeks, and her eyes were overly bright. She was wearing her coat, a rose knit scarf around her throat. "This isn't going to work. This isn't right, not for me, not anymore."

She slipped her wedding ring off her finger and tried to hand it to Jet, but he wouldn't take it and she leaned past him, placing it on the table edge, right next to Miss Warner's place setting. "I've got my things and I'm heading out. I'll be back for Judas as soon as I can, which will probably be when the snow melts." She nodded at them and then walked out, picking up her suitcase and backpack, and carried them through the entry and out the front door.

The door closed almost gently behind her.

Jet had no idea what was going on. He glanced at Cade baffled, unsure what had just happened. Briar was leaving him?

Why?

What had he done?

Jet reached for the gold band she'd set on the table, his hand closing around it. The ring was still warm. He could almost feel it on her finger, reminding him of how he'd turned it, around and around as they talked. She belonged in his arms, belonged in his life, the ring on her finger as they talked late in the night, making plans for a future. Counting the stars.

"Go talk to her," Cade said roughly. "Briar shouldn't be driving in this weather. Her truck is old, and the roads are covered in ice."

It was all Jet could do to not punch Cade in the face. "I know," he gritted, grabbing his hat and heading after her. "I know how to love her."

Jet ran toward the barn but stopped short when he saw Briar's truck still parked near the other ranch trucks.

So, she wasn't leaving, good. Then where was she?

Jet headed to Cade's cabin. MerriBee answered the door and shook her head when he asked if Briar was there.

Jet went to the bunkhouse next, but no Briar there, either.

Then one of the young guys, a new guy who'd just been hired in the last week, mentioned seeing Briar taking Judas out. She'd saddled him for a ride.

Jet thanked him and swore under his breath as he looked up at the sky with the heavy storm clouds, more snow on the way, how could she head out on her own now?

He wasn't about to take a horse now when everything was so icy. Even he knew how dangerous it was. A horse could slip, fall, roll on the rider, or panic, rear up, and throw the rider. There were countless ways to get hurt on a day like today and it blew his mind that Briar would take such a risk, and not just with herself, but the baby, too.

He jumped on one of the ATVs and took off, hoping to catch up with her. He scanned the horizon, his gaze sweeping the pasture, the distant fields, the hills, the snow-covered road.

Anything could happen out here and once the snow started to fall there would be no way to track footprints.

Why would she do this? What was she thinking?

He swallowed his fear, angry with himself, angry with her. He was scared for her, but he wasn't going to think the worst. Judas was sure footed. Briar rode well. Nothing was going to happen. She'd turn around soon and return to the barn frozen and stiff, but ultimately fine.

And yet how could she be so impulsive?

How could she not realize how vulnerable she was, and how dependent her baby was on Briar, needing Briar to make good decisions? Wise decisions—

He stood up on the pedals, his attention caught by a dark spot in the distance, a brown mound against the pristine snow.

Judas. But Judas didn't seem to be moving, and Jet sped across the pasture, trying to see where Briar was, because she wasn't on his back, and then only after he'd traveled farther, he realized Judas wasn't on his feet. He was lying on his side in the snow. And there was Briar next to him, cradling Judas's head.

Jet parked, turned off the engine and jogged through the snow. Briar was nearly hysterical. "He's hurt his leg. He went down. It's my fault—" She broke off, face ashen, eyes enormous. "You have to help him, Jet. Please. Please."

Jet knew math and science; he knew how to fight and fly a plane. But he didn't know horses, and he didn't know what had happened but whatever occurred, it was serious.

"Listen to me," he said, crouching next to Briar. "The only way I can help him, is if you help me. You have to ride the ATV back, follow my trail, go back, get Cade, tell him to call a vet, tell him to get a horse trailer, tell him to get as many guys as possible."

"But how will you get a horse trailer back here? How will you get him out of here?"

"I don't know, but Cade might. So, pull yourself together and head back and get help. I'll stay with Judas."

"Why can't I stay? What if he dies?"

He moved closer, his knees touching hers. He brushed a snowflake from her eyebrow. "You can't stay out here," he said quietly. "You have a baby to think of—"

"Judas is my baby, too. He's been mine far longer."

"Briar, love, everyone is going to do what they can, and maybe we can save Judas, and maybe we can't, but how will it make anything better if you lose both your babies today?"

Something he said seemed to penetrate her brain as she lifted her head and searched his eyes.

"Is that a risk you're truly prepared to take?" he added. Time was of the essence. She needed to go get help now, and she needed to do it quickly, but safely, so she didn't end up hurt.

Briar kissed Judas and then got to her feet. "How will Cade know where to find you?"

"Tell him the west pasture. He should take the west

road, too. It would allow truck and equipment to get close."

※

Miss Warner, MerriBee, and Grace kept Briar company while Cade and the ranch hands descended on the west pasture.

Emma carried in a tray of cookies and hot coffee and tea. No one took anything, except for Grace who wanted a sugar cookie while she played with the basket of antique blocks MerriBee had brought out from the downstairs hall closet.

"I hate myself," Briar whispered, knotting and unknotting her hands. "This is all my fault. I took him out so I could calm down and clear my head. I realized I was too upset, too emotional, and I didn't want to storm off. That's what I might have done in the past. I didn't want to do it this time. I wanted to be smart—" She broke off. "Instead I injured Judas."

Miss Warner and MerriBee exchanged glances. Briar saw the look, saw their expression. They pitied her. They didn't think Judas's outcome would be good.

She said nothing else, unable to speak, and was grateful no one tried to console her or give her false hope. It was very rare when a horse recovered from a broken leg. And once a horse went down the way Judas did, it would be almost impossible to get him on the stretcher without further injuring him.

Emma returned later, asked Miss Warner if she'd like

some soup or lunch. Miss Warner shook her head. MerriBee glanced at her watch, and noting the time, scooped up Grace to go feed her, leaving Briar and Miss Warner alone.

Time passed, slowly, agonizingly and it felt like hours before Willis entered the house and appeared in the living room doorway saying Cade thought Briar should come down to the barn.

Briar grabbed her coat from the mudroom, but her hands were shaking so much she couldn't zip the jacket closed.

Emma had been watching from the kitchen and she crossed to Briar and helped with the zipper. "No matter what happens," Emma said quietly, giving Briar a hug, "you have given him a wonderful life, you've shown him so much love."

Briar couldn't answer. Numbly, she followed Willis out, trudging behind him, stepping in his steps, taking advantage of the compacted snow.

There were trucks and a huge van parked in front of the barn. She assumed one was the veterinarian's but didn't know the rest. She glanced at Willis but couldn't read anything from his expression. Why did cowboys have to be so stoic?

Cade was the first to see Briar enter the barn and he came to her.

"Tell me he's not dead." She choked trying to see past him, trying to see Judas, and make sense of all the activity.

"He's not dead," Cade said.

"His leg? Is it broken?"

"No. He stumbled because he's sick. His belly is distended. The doctor thinks it's salmonella. He's taken samples now and will be taking them to the lab. In the meantime, Judas is getting fluids and we'll get him on antibiotics and try to keep him comfortable."

"How did he get it? It doesn't make sense."

"Probably from the new hire's horse." He must have seen she didn't understand. "The vet thinks it's possible Tar, Ray's horse, has been shedding the bacteria without anyone knowing, spreading the bacteria from one horse to another by using the same shovel to muck stalls."

"Has any other horse showed signs of illness?"

"Miss Warner's."

"Oh, no. Miss Warner loves that horse."

"I'm doing everything I can to save both."

She shook her head. "I thought I'd killed him. I thought—" She broke off, tears not far off. "Can I go see him?"

"No."

Her head jerked up. "Why not? What's happening to him?"

"Nothing, but Briar, salmonella can be passed to humans. With you pregnant, we can't have you near him. Maybe later after we've cleaned the barn thoroughly, disinfecting everything, we could get you near him, but you're going to have to be careful. There are risks."

Her eyes burned as she struggled to take it all in. She hadn't hurt Judas. Judas was sick. But she couldn't go comfort him. She couldn't help care for him.

"Briar," Cade said gently, "I know how much you love that horse. We all do. We're going to take care of him for you. I'm going to take care of him for you. Nothing will happen to him on my watch. I swear to you. I know I've let you down, I know you're disappointed in me, but I won't let you down again. Leave Judas to me. We'll get him better. I promise." He gave her a hug and then added, "Now go shower and make sure Emma knows that everything you're wearing needs to be washed on the sanitize cycle."

BRIAR RETURNED TO the house. Emma met her at the door. "How is he?" Emma asked.

"Cade says he's going to be alright. He promised me."

"I'm so glad to hear it. Now, what can I get you?"

"Nothing. I have to shower. I have germs on me."

"Let me get you my special soap. It'll kill everything but not the environment."

"Sounds like a good soap."

Emma bustled off, returning a minute later with a plastic bottle. "Leave this in your shower. Jet will probably want to use it if it's something from the barn."

"It is. Willis will need to be washing in it, too."

"Good thing I have a lot."

Briar struggled to smile. "I'd hug you but the germs…"

"An air hug then," Emma said, arms out, hugging air. "Oh! Your bags are back in your room. MerriBee took them up." Emma's eyes widened. "I better take some soap to Cade and his crew, too."

"And the bunkhouse," Briar said. "Everyone needs to get disinfected."

"Sounds like I need to buy more."

AFTER THE SHOWER, and the very liberal use of soap on her body and her hair, Briar put on clean clothes and dried her hair, using the hair dryer's hottest setting to make sure she'd killed every bit of bacteria that might have survived the soap and scrubbing.

Dinner was soon, but Briar couldn't imagine putting on proper clothes and going down to eat. She couldn't imagine talking to anyone or listening to polite conversation. She was just too tired. Today, it was all too much.

She was pulling back the duvet when Jet entered the room, after a knock on the door.

"Everyone's gathered in the living room," he said, his hair damp, his jaw clean shaven. He obviously showered but she didn't know where. "I'm to escort you down."

"I don't think I can handle dinner tonight," she answered, climbing into bed, relishing the coolness of the sheets and the softness of the feather mattress topper that made the bed feel so good.

"You have to eat."

"I don't have to eat."

"Fine. But you have to come down. Everyone is waiting for you."

"Jet, not tonight. It's been a terrible day."

"I'm right there with you. You wouldn't believe my day. My wife left me. She nearly froze to death. Her horse nearly died. I spent hours scrubbing a horse stall, cleaning salmonella—"

"Okay, you're right." She flung the covers back and got out of bed. "But your wife didn't leave you. She just... needed to clear her head."

"Is that what it was?"

"Yes. She heard you and Cade arguing and she was afraid Cade would fire you, so if she just left, things would be better."

"That's not how love works."

She froze, stunned. "You know I love you?"

He smiled at her, heat in his eyes. "I know I love you. I'm wildly in love with you—"

"You're not," she protested.

His smile grew. "Sorry, sweetheart, I am."

"Since when?"

"Since I met you."

Briar couldn't believe it. "Impossible. You didn't even

like me."

"That's not true," he said, tugging her closer, bringing her into his arms. "You were young, beautiful, and trouble—"

"Exactly. And then you found out I was in a situation."

"You probably will always be in a situation but that's just your charm."

"I should object to that," she said, but as Jet's lips were on her neck, pressing kisses to a very sensitive spot, she couldn't concentrate on anything but the delicious tingling shivers racing down her spine. "Um, why do we have to go downstairs again?"

"They want to celebrate us. Emma spent all afternoon making a cake."

"Oh, Jet, I can't."

"Why?" he asked, lifting his head to look into her eyes.

"I don't know where my ring is. It's not on the dining room table. I checked."

Jet reached into his pocket and pulled the simple gold band out. "I have it. Let me see your hand." He slid the ring onto her finger and then kissed her. "I know you're tired, so we'll keep it a short night."

She looked down at the band, glad to have it back on her hand where it belonged. "I won't do that again. I was trying to make a point and it was stupid."

"It wasn't stupid. You were being dramatic. There's a difference."

She fought her smile. "You're laughing at me."

"I find you delightful."

"*Mmm*, I'm sure."

He kissed her again, kissing her until she was breathless and dizzy and clinging to him for support. "Should we go downstairs?" he murmured, lifting his head. "Have our celebration cake and sneak back up?"

She looked up into his intensely blue eyes, her middle still filled with butterflies. "Only if you promise to kiss me again when we return."

"I promise," he said solemnly.

She laughed and stood up on tiptoe to press a kiss to his lips. "Jet Manning, I love you."

"I love you, too, Mrs. Manning."

DOWNSTAIRS, THEY ENTERED the living room and discovered a party. A petite wedding cake sat on a round table flanked by a bottle of champagne and antique flutes and dessert plates. Ace and Rolly were acting as waiters, passing around appetizers. Willis snagged an appetizer and popped it in his mouth as Emma smoothed his dress shirt, knocking away crumbs. Cade and MerriBee were trying to soothe a grumpy, fussing Grace and Miss Warner sat silent and pensive by the fire.

But when Emma spotted Briar and Jet walking in, hand in hand, she let out a cheer. Miss Warner suddenly sat up and smiled. Willis reached for the champagne bottle and popped the cork. Startled, Grace let out a wail, crying in earnest.

Briar glanced at Jet and smiled. He leaned over and kissed her in front of everyone. Miss Warner pushed up out of her chair and lifted her hands to get everyone's attention. "Cade, do you want to share the news, or should I?"

"You do it," Cade said, putting his arm around Merri-Bee.

"But it was your idea," Miss Warner said, voice quavering, "and Briar should know that."

Briar glanced up at Jet to see if he knew what was going on, but he gave his head a shake, just as confused as she was.

"I don't want to lose you two," Miss Warner said, looking at Briar and Jet. "But I've quickly realized this ranch isn't big enough for everyone, not with you all starting families. So, after Cade returned from the barn, and goodness how terribly upsetting all that has been, he and I talked about what would be best for the Mannings, the Hunts, and the Warners, and it's been my plan since acquiring the Gilstrap Ranch to have Jet there, onsite managing the property."

She paused and smiled at Cade. "But Cade had a better idea. He thought perhaps we carve out a section, perhaps where the farmhouse currently is, and deed it to Briar and Jet so you'd have a home and Briar could have her stable, and Jet could still oversee the farm."

She stopped talking and clasped her hands. "Obviously, you're under no obligation to accept. Think about it tonight and tomorrow. Take a week, it doesn't matter to me. We just want you to know we love you both and want you near, if such an arrangement appealed to you."

Willis began pouring champagne into the delicate handblown heirloom flutes. Emma handed the cake knife to Briar and Jet, insisting they cut their cake together and then she wanted them to feed each other just like at a proper reception.

They were cheered as they fed each other, and then cheered and toasted by Cade and Willis, and a brief happy toast by MerriBee. The cowboy waiters were sneaking champagne and Miss Warner just watched it all, tired but pleased.

And then Miss Warner said she hated to break up the party, but she had to call it a night. Briar went to help clean up but Willis shooed her away, saying he would be helping Emma and Briar should take her man upstairs and enjoy her honeymoon.

Blushing, Briar retrieved Jet from where he was talking to Ace and, taking him by the hand, she pulled him up the stairs and down the hall to their room.

But once inside the room she didn't want to kiss, she didn't want to sleep, she had to find out what Jet was thinking. "I couldn't tell from your expression if you liked the idea of managing the Gilstrap Farm, or if you'd seen the old farmhouse and if there was a stable there or any of it."

He sat down on the bed and patted the space next to

him. "I knew they were going to hire a manager for the farm. I'd hoped they'd consider me, but I hadn't discussed the opportunity with Cade yet, only briefly with Miss Warner."

"The farmhouse ... it's livable?"

"It has good bones. It could use some work but nothing that scares me."

She smiled. "Nothing scares you anyway."

"I do like to be challenged."

"So, this is a good thing?" she pressed.

"I'm very interested. There are significant pluses."

"We'd have our own place," she said.

"And I'd have my own work, and a great deal more independence."

"So, what are the drawbacks?"

He lay back and drew her down so she curled against him. "You'd be away from Cade," he said. "As well as Miss Warner and Emma."

"But I'd have you."

He smiled at her and caressed her back, starting at her nape and running his hand down to the small of her spine. "I don't want you to get lonely, and with the baby coming, you might feel trapped."

"I grew up on a ranch with nothing around for miles. I like living on the land, and I very much like us having our own place. Our own home." She tried to picture the house and then the property. "There must be a barn."

"Yes, and plenty of space to build a proper stable one

day. If we're happy there. If we want to stay."

"They're just giving us land and a house. Why?"

"I believe there are some tax benefits for the Warner Trust, and then there is Cade's desire to have his beloved little sister settled near him so his kids can grow up with cousins nearby."

A lump filled her throat. For a moment she couldn't speak. She swallowed once, and again. "It seems too good to be true."

"It's a very generous wedding present," he agreed.

"How do we say no?"

Jet kissed her. "We don't. Not unless there's something else you'd rather do?"

"No. I love this. All of it. I love the idea of starting fresh here and building a life with you." She smiled into his eyes, unbelievably, deliriously happy. "When can we go see the house?"

"As soon as we can plow the entrance to the Gilstrap Farm road."

Epilogue

It was early June and summer had finally arrived in the Big Horn Mountains. Briar and Jet had been living in the old farmhouse on what used to be the Gilstrap Ranch for over a month and every day it grew warmer, and Briar felt a little bigger, but she'd never been so happy in her life.

While Jet poured his energy into the farm, Briar did her best to learn everything she could about hay and alfalfa. She visited the Johnson County Library in Buffalo and checked out books and magazines reading up so she could help Jet as much as possible. Not that he asked for help, but if she was going to be a farmer's wife, she should know something about crops and rotation and mowing fields.

One morning, waking early, she picked up the yellowed magazine from the side of her bed and tried to finish reading the article she'd started last night. Jet woke up and slid his hand under the cover to rub her tummy, his way of saying good morning to baby girl every day.

She smiled and stretched, loving the feel of his hand on her. "Can I read you something?" she asked him. "It's about hay."

"Then by all means, read."

"It's from an article in the 1920 issue of *The Encampment Echo*, about best management practices for the small hay grower." She glanced over at him. "But we're not small hay growers, are we?"

His lips curved. "No, we're not, but I am intrigued."

Briar cleared her throat and began reading in her most professional voice. "*The small hay grower, however, need not make a very heavy investment in new haying apparatus, for by rearranging the working of his crew and using a little more horse labor for the hard work he can add considerably to the efficiency of his crew.*" She turned the page. "Should I continue?"

"Please."

"*First, do not run two or more mowers close together. If the front mower has any trouble causing it to stop, all of the mowers usually wait while repairs are made on one.*" Briar skimmed the paragraph and moved on to something she thought Jet would find interesting. "*There is a tendency for drivers to waste too much time talking when they stop occasionally to let the teams rest. A good practice when two or more machines are used is for each driver to work independently, so there will be no interference from other machines.*"

She looked up at him. "So, no talking on the job. And no having fun, either."

"That was then, and this is now, and work shouldn't be miserable. I happen to love my job." Jet gave her a kiss, and left the bed, heading into the bathroom to shower and shave.

"Any plans for the day?" he asked her fifteen minutes later, emerging from the bathroom nearly dressed.

Briar put down the magazine. "I'm going to go see Miss Warner this morning and then I have a checkup this afternoon."

"I thought you had a checkup last week."

"It's every week now until she arrives." Briar hesitated. "Jet, I have a serious question for you."

He'd been buttoning his work shirt and his hands stilled. "Okay."

"I think we should get married."

His eyebrow quirked. "Sweetheart, in case there's any confusion, we *are* married."

She laughed. "But *really* married."

He crossed to her and sat down on the edge of the mattress, resting his hand on her hip. "We have a marriage license. The paperwork is finalized. It's legal."

"But my dad couldn't be there. And Cade and Bee and Miss Warner couldn't be there."

She searched his eyes. "I thought if we had another ceremony, my dad could give me away. It would mean a lot to him, I think, and it would mean a lot to me."

His expression cleared. "I have another idea," he said.

"Oh?"

"Why doesn't Cade give you away and your father marry us?"

She slowly smiled. "I like that even better."

"So, when would this happen, before little Katherine arrives, or after?"

"Oh, before. Definitely before. My dad and Cade aren't that modern."

"How do we plan a wedding in oh, two or three weeks?"

"It's a small wedding and you wear whatever you want—you're always gorgeous—and I'll find something here in town. In fact, I saw a dress in the prom and bridal store. It's pink with lots of tulle and a gorgeous big bow at the back."

"It sounds beautiful but it's not a maternity design, is it?"

"No, but it's really pretty and Emma is so talented she'd know how to make it fit."

"You really want to do this."

She reached for his hand and held it. "I want to marry you again, because I want to marry you, not because I have to."

"You never had to marry me, Briar."

"I know, but this is different. This is me asking you to spend the rest of your life with me."

"So where do we marry? In town, here? Invite all twelve of our friends to dance in our new stable and barn complex?"

"First of all, there are twenty-four if we let Cade include all of the Wyatts, and secondly, I'm not sure Judas would like anyone near his new stable. Ever since Tar gave him salmonella, he's very picky about the company he keeps."

"Then how about where we met?" Jet said. "It's beautiful at the Sundowner this time of year. We could have the ceremony on the ridge just before sunset with the Big Horn Mountains behind us."

She kissed his hand. "You're very romantic, Mr. Manning."

"That's because I love you, Mrs. Manning." He smiled into her eyes. "You are beautiful. I'm lucky to have you."

"We're lucky to have each other."

Jet hesitated. "Just promise me if we do this, you're not going to go into labor early. We've had enough excitement this spring. I'd like to at least stick with our birth plan."

"I agree. There's no way our little Katherine is going to ruin this wedding."

※

BUT LITTLE KATHERINE had a mind of her own.

Two weeks later they were on the mountain, the sun dropping behind them, painting the sky glorious shades of peach and pink as Jet and Briar recited their vows and then received their blessing from Briar's father. Just as Patrick Phillips pronounced them man and wife, Briar gasped, her hand pressing against her side.

"Jet," she whispered. "I think she's coming."

"Now?" he said.

"Now." She clutched his arm, feeling the water trickling down her leg. "Oh, Jet, no. This can't be happening. I don't want to give birth up here."

Fortunately for Briar, Katherine Warner Manning was good enough to wait an hour and make her formal appearance in the labor and delivery room at the Johnson County Healthcare Center. The delivery was so fast there was no time for an epidural and Katherine, or little Katie, in honor of Jet's mom, emerged pink and healthy and screaming at the top of her lungs.

Tears filled Briar's eyes as she was handed her little girl swaddled in a pale pink blanket. "Welcome to the world, Katie Manning," she whispered, kissing her daughter's dark head. "Mama loves you forever and ever, and I will be here for you for always."

Jet leaned over and kissed Briar and then tiny Katie's forehead. "Katie, I will be here, too, especially for your Goth phase. I'm looking forward to that."

Briar laughed, feeling so much joy and peace. It had been a long time coming but her world was complete.

Jet couldn't look away from Briar's face. He kissed her tenderly, adding, "Love you, my beautiful Briar. Not sure if you know this, but I wasn't the hero in this story. You were. You, my fierce, brave girl, rescued me."

She smiled up into his blue eyes. "We saved each other, I think."

"And now we have our Katie."

"Maybe in another year or two we'll give her a brother or

sister? I hated being an only child. I don't want her to be one, either."

"I couldn't agree more."

THE END

See where it all began in
MONTANA COWBOY ROMANCE!

Can Ella and Baird both keep their distance or will the magic of the Christmas season bring these two together? Find out in THE CHRISTMAS COTTAGE, releasing in December 2023!

THE WYATT BROTHERS OF MONTANA SERIES

Book 1: *Montana Cowboy Romance*

Book 2: *Montana Cowboy Christmas*

Book 3: *Montana Cowboy Daddy*

Book 4: *Montana Cowboy Miracle*

Book 5: *Montana Cowboy Promise*

Book 6: *Montana Cowboy Bride*

Available now at your favorite online retailer!

More by Jane Porter

Oh, Christmas Night

Love at Langley Park series

Book 1: *Once Upon a Christmas*

Book 2: *The Christmas Cottage*
Coming in December 2023!

Love on Chance Avenue series

Book 1: *Take Me, Cowboy*
Winner of the RITA® Award for Best Romance Novella

Book 2: *Miracle on Chance Avenue*

Book 3: *Take a Chance on Me*

Book 4: *Not Christmas Without You*

The Taming of the Sheenans series

The Sheenans are six powerful wealthy brothers from Marietta, Montana. They are big, tough, rugged men, and as different as the Montana landscape.

Christmas at Copper Mountain
Book 1: Brock Sheenan's story

The Tycoon's Kiss
Book 2: Troy Sheenan's story

The Kidnapped Christmas Bride
Book 3: Trey Sheenan's story

The Taming of the Bachelor
Book 4: Dillion Sheenan's story

A Christmas Miracle for Daisy
Book 5: Cormac Sheenan's story

The Lost Sheenan's Bride
Book 6: Shane Sheenan's story

Available now at your favorite online retailer!

About the Author

New York Times and USA Today bestselling author of 70 romances and fiction titles, **Jane Porter** has been a finalist for the prestigious RITA award six times and won in 2014 for Best Novella with her story, *Take Me, Cowboy*, from Tule Publishing. Today, Jane has over 13 million copies in print, including her wildly successful, *Flirting With Forty*, which was made into a Lifetime movie starring Heather Locklear, as well as *The Tycoon's Kiss* and *A Christmas Miracle for Daisy*, two Tule books which have been turned into holiday films for the GAC Family network. A mother of three sons, Jane holds an MA in Writing from the University of San Francisco and makes her home in sunny San Clemente, CA with her surfer husband and three dogs.

Thank you for reading

Montana Cowboy Bride

If you enjoyed this book, you can find more from all our great authors at TulePublishing.com, or from your favorite online retailer.

Printed in Great Britain
by Amazon